GREEN DAY REVEALED

Publisher and Creative Director: Nick Wells
Project Editor and Picture Research: Chelsea Edwards
Art Director and Layout Design: Mike Spender
Digital Design and Production: Chris Herbert
Proofreader: Amanda Leigh
Indexer: Geoffrey Meadon

Special thanks to: Giana Porpiglia, Polly Prior and Digby Smith

First published 2011 by
FLAME TREE PUBLISHING
Crabtree Hall, Crabtree Lane
Fulham, London SW6 6TY
United Kingdom

www.flametreepublishing.com
Music information site: www.flametreemusic.com

Flame Tree is part of the Foundry Creative Media Company Ltd
© 2011 The Foundry

11 13 15 14 12
1 3 5 7 9 8 6 4 2

The CIP record for this book is available from the British Library.

ISBN: 978-0-85775-147-8

IAN SHIRLEY (Author) lived and pogoed his way through British punk rock and has been buying records and watching bands ever since. He is an experienced music journalist whose feature work and reviews appear in respected magazines like *Record Collector* and *Goldmine*. He was written the biographies of Bauhaus and The Residents as well as two science-fiction novels. He has also written the definitive tome on the links between comics and music: *Can Rock And Roll Save The World?*, and contributed to Flame Tree's *The Definitive Illustrated Encyclopedia of Rock*. He is currently the editor of *Record Collector's Rare Record Price Guide* and has a collection of over 2,000 vinyl albums, 4,000 45rpm singles and 5,000 CDs.

JOHN HOLMSTROM (Foreword) In 1975 John Holmstrom founded *Punk* magazine. Its hand-lettered graphics inspired many other fanzines, launched the punk rock movement and helped create 'Punk Art,' a short-lived movement that inspired the East Village art scene a few years later. Holmstrom later started the comic 'zines *Comical Funnies* and *Stop!* and designed posters, t-shirts as well as record, book and CD covers, and contributed to dozens of publications such as *Bananas*, *High Times* and *Heavy Metal*. He's currently working on *The Best of Punk Magazine* for Harper Books.

Picture Credits

Alamy Images: 50, Travel Division Images: 83 (r). © **Gregory Bojorquez:** 112. © **Murray Bowles:** 4 (l), 15, 16, 18, 19 (r), 21, 23, 24, 25, 28, 29, 32. **Camera Press:** 153 (t), 154. **Corbis:** Sygma: 74, 75, 77; John Atashian: 88; Rune Hellestad: 91, 113; Anthony Pidgeon/Retna Ltd: 98; Mike Laye: 117; Kevin Estrada/Retna Ltd: 162; Walter McBride/Retna Ltd: 177; Walter McBride: 185; ERIC LUSE/San Francisco Chronicle: 42(t); LGI Stock: 53 (t). **Courtesy of Harmonix:** 178. **Foundry Arts:** 14 (b), 19 (l), 35 (br), 42 (b), 53 (b), 71, 83 (l), 87 (tl), 95 (c), 120 (b), 153 (b), 156, 181 (b). **Getty Images:** Nigel Crane/Redferns: 3, 158; Joe Kohen/WireImage: 3, 160; Graham Knowles/Redferns: 5 (l), 101; Tim Mosenfelder: 6, 87 (c), 103; Robert Knight Archive/Redferns: 8, 26; Dave Hogan/Stringer/Getty Images for MTV: 9, 130; Christina Radish/Redferns: 10, 102; Catherine McGann/Archive Photos: 39, 43; Ken Schles/Time & Life Pictures: 40; Jim Steinfeldt/Michael Ochs Archives: 44, 67; Ebet Roberts/Redferns: 48; Bob Berg: 55; Tim Mosenfelder: 56; Paul Bergen/Redferns: 57; Tim Mosenfelder: 81; David Teuma: 82; Jeff Kravitz/FimMagic Inc.: 89, 186; Clay Patrick McBride/Premium Archive: 92; Ross Gimore/Redferns: 94; Jon Super/Redferns: 95 (r), 105, 106; L. Cohen/WireImage: 96; Teresa Lee/Stringer: 100; KMazur/WireImage: 104; Kevin Kane/WireImage: 108, 138; Steve Jennings/WireImage: 120 (t); KMazur/WireImage: 123, 125; Frank Micelotta: 126, 128; Jeff Kravitz/Stringer/FilmMagic, Inc.: 131; Dave Etheridge-Barnes: 132; Peter Still/Redferns: 134; Louise Wilson: 136; Kurt Vinion/WireImage: 137; Kevin Winter: 141; John Sciulli/WireImage: 142; Martin Philbey/Redferns: 143; John Shearer/WireImage: 144, 145, 168; Lester Cohen/WireImage: 148; Chris Graythen/Stringer: 149; J Ross: 150; Frank Mullen/WireImage: 155; Stephen Albanese/Michael Ochs Archives: 165; Michael Loccisano: 166; Nick Harvey/WireImage: 169; Matt Kent/WireImage: 170; Kevin Mazur/WireImage: 172; Jeff Kravitz/AMA2009/FilmMagic: 174; Kevork Djansezian: 175; Kevin Mazur/WireImage: 176; AFP/Stringer: 180; Andrew H. Walker: 181 (t); Scott Legato/FilmMagic: 182; C. Flanigan/FilmMagic: 184; Buda Mendes: 188. © **Dean Chalkley/NME/IPC+ Syndication:** 121. **PA Photos:** Rich Pedroncelli/AP: 14 (t); Suzan Moore/EMPICS Entertainment: 62; JK/EMPICS Entertainment: 80, 90; Yui Mok/PA Archive: 124. **Photofest:** Atlantic Records/Photofest: 35 (c); 4 (m), 36, 38, 68, 152. **Photoshot:** Starstock: 86. **Record covers:** courtesy of Reprise Records, a Warner Music Group Company. **Retna:** Jay Blakesberg: 1, 4 (r), 5 (l), 11, 37, 60, 69, 70, 72, 97, 116, 118, 133, 140, 164; John Popplewell: 33, 34; Scott Weiner: 46, 54; Zsolt Sarvary: 49; Gary Gershoff: 51; Bob Ramirez: 64; Steve Jennings: 76; Pamela Littky: 114; Dennis Van Tine: 157 **Shutterstock:** Corky Buczyk: 79. Cover Courtesy of **Rolling Stone** Issue Dated December 28, 1995 (Photo by Mark Seliger) © Rolling Stone, LLC 1995 All Rights Reserved. Printed By Permission: 61. Record companies, artists, photographers and designers retain the copyright for cover images.

Printed in China

GREEN DAY REVEALED

BY IAN SHIRLEY
FOREWORD BY JOHN HOLMSTROM

FLAME TREE
PUBLISHING

CONTENTS

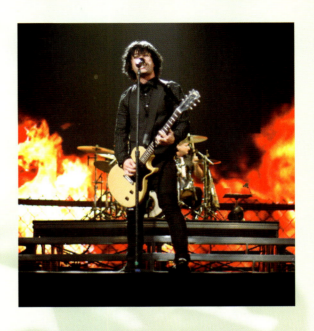

FOREWORD

I remember it like it was last week: I was hanging around the art department at HiGH TiMES magazine in late 1994 when an advertisement from a record company came in. A bunch of us were eager to see it since few rock bands had the guts to support us back then. The advertisement featured a funny cartoon illustration, which of course I always appreciate, with 'Dookie' and 'Green Day' in big letters on it. I'd never heard of the band, 'Dookie', and had no idea what they meant by calling their album 'Green Day', but I liked their image. Unfortunately, Dookie didn't send a review CD along with their ad, so I figured it was just another hippie jam band.

A few weeks later I visited my big sister Anne who, as a teenager, introduced me to everything cool that shaped my life: The Beatles, MAD magazine, elephant jokes, etc. She had news about her son Matt, who had just turned fifteen: 'Would you believe it? He likes punk rock music! So all he wants for Christmas is a guitar and an amplifier.' (And yes, cool person my big sis is, he got 'em!)

I was so proud of him! Matt was eager to talk music with me, since I had worked with The Ramones and all. Suddenly I was 'the cool uncle' instead of 'the loser uncle'.

So I asked Matt, 'Who are your favourite punk bands?'

'Only two: The Ramones and Green Day!'

'Green Day? Um, yeah – I've heard… I've heard of Green Day.'

'They're so cool! One of their songs is about…,' Matt lowered his voice so his parents couldn't hear, 'Jacking off!' Then he laughed hysterically. I figured, 'This band has to be great! They understand the whole teenager thing! How punk rock can you get?'

When I got home I picked up a bunch of Green Day CDs, and instantly liked the band. They had a nice, smooth sound, the songs were simple, fast, loud, energetic and pop, the musicians were good but not trying to be virtuoso and the singer had a pleasant voice. And of course, they didn't take themselves too seriously.

I was surprised to see that classic, Ramones-style punk rock was being revived. Since my magazine PUNK, which helped ignite the scene in 1976, folded in 1979 I hadn't paid a whole lot of attention to the music. Once the 1980s arrived, hardcore punk took over and most of it was too political and serious for me. Besides, I always thought rock'n'roll was supposed to attract females, and too many hardcore bands seemed to enjoy those hot, sweaty mosh pits, filled with dozens of half-naked young men bumping bodies and pushing flesh into flesh… Green Day seemed liberated from that whole mess. Punk was fun again!

Soon, Green Day became impossible to ignore! I heard 'Welcome to Paradise' everywhere, everyone talked about the famous mud-fight at Woodstock 1994, and everyone seemed to like them.

People seemed to like them less after their next albums, INSOMNIA (which for some reason I liked better than DOOKIE, but who knows) and NIMROD, which scored a major hit with 'Good Riddance (Time Of Your Life)', which is inevitable whenever a band become rock superstars. (Especially when a punk rock band become so popular, just ask Blondie.) They were always receiving awards and stuff, which is also way out of the ordinary for a punk rock band.

The backlash against them just went on, even though, but probably because, they continued to be the mainstream face of punk rock. Haters would say, 'A REAL punk rock band wouldn't appear on MTV!' (Well, you know, The Ramones always hoped they could be on MTV, which is why they bothered to make so many videos.) But I still kind of liked Green Day since at least punk was still alive! And when I saw them on KING OF THE HILL in 1997 I thought it was very cool, since so many great 1960s bands appeared on sitcoms like GILLIGAN'S ISLAND or THE MUNSTERS.

By the time Green Day collaborated with Iggy Pop on 'Skull Ring' in 2003, I think most of the haters were being won over. No one could say they hadn't paid some dues by now, and one thing in punk rock will always be true: 'You can't argue with Iggy.' I mean, you can try, but if Iggy lets you in his club...' Enough said. (Of course, there's always an exception to the rule, in this case: Madonna.)

Then came AMERICAN IDIOT, one of those amazing records that define history and redefine music. It hit No. 1! It swept the MTV Music Awards! Now AMERICAN IDIOT is a Broadway musical. As I write this Billie Joe Armstrong himself is appearing on Broadway! (By the way, I think this is very cool, since back in 1973 the first punk rock band I fever idolized, Alice Cooper, tried to stage shows on The Great White Way, but I guess the world wasn't ready for it yet.)

By the way, I heard a strong rumour that Green Day were going to perform live at CBGBs during the MTV Music Video Awards in September 2005, in support of the Save CBGB campaign, but Hurricane Katrina changed everyone's plans and cancelled the show since it hit Miami, where the event took place, before slamming into New Orleans and causing one of the worst tragedies in American history. Who knows? Maybe they could have saved CBGBs.

Well, okay, all of you Green Day fans can remember their other career highlights much better than me. I am not a fan, just an old-timer who appreciates their music and what they've contributed to the rock scene over the years. Believe me, it's not easy to do what they've done, otherwise a lot more people would have done it. They got to the top just a few years after forming in 1987, and have stayed there ever since, and have made good music and have stayed interesting for 25 years.

I don't care what anyone says, Green Day were and are punk rock in all the best ways. Sure, over time they've grown musically, no band can stay the same forever. The important fact to me is that Green Day have been one of the few bands to keep rock'n'roll alive. They used to say in the 1950s 'Rock'N'Roll will never die!' and today, that's still true. Don't hate them because they're popular, celebrate them instead.

JOHN HOLMSTROM
New York

INTRODUCTION

In March 2011 the NEW MUSICAL EXPRESS published a list of the Top 100 gigs that music fans 'should have been at'. Green Day were at No. 68 and the gig in question was their famed performance at The Den in Wigan on 21 December 1991 where they not only performed tracks from their debut LP 39/SMOOTH and upcoming album KERPLUNK but also took part in an improvised nativity play. Although I was, sadly, not at this gig, a good friend saw Green Day perform a few days earlier in a small London venue in front of around 90 people. Appearing on the same bill were Wat Tyler and headliners Jailcell Recipes, both of whom he preferred to the unknown American punks. Perhaps he should have paid more attention to the trio, whose journey from playing in front of 90 to rocking giant stadia is a truly remarkable one.

Green Day were inspired to make music by the punk movement that emerged in America in the late 1980s and early 1990s. It took hold in their native Bay Area and was intensified by the famed Gilman Street Project, a co-operative venue which not only helped establish local heroes like Operation Ivy but also gave succour to a host of new bands of which Green Day were one. Although they now live in multi-million dollar homes, Green Day started out playing any venue that would take them, from house parties to squats in Europe where payment was a little money, food, something more than tobacco to smoke and a bed for the night. Musically, although they drew water from established punk and hardcore bands, main songwriter Billie Joe Armstrong also had a tentacle in other musical pockets such as the melodic throb of The Buzzcocks. Their early material demonstrates this musical variety. Many of the tracks on 39/SMOOTH, such as 'The Judge's Daughter', had a clean accessibility; this diversity is also what gives the music its immediate resonance today.

Green Day signed to Reprise Records in the wake of Nirvana's proclamation that, after the success of their seminal NEVERMIND (1991), independent rock music could sell millions of units. Many who belonged to the movement that spawned them saw this as an abandonment of their punk principles, and led to spiteful fanzine editorials and constant interview questions from probing journalists about 'selling out'. It could be fair to say that after two EPs and two LPs on Lookout!, Green Day had taken the independent route as far as it could go at a time when, as a live band, they were reaching critical mass and needed better support and marketing for their records. That their third album DOOKIE (1994) went on to sell over 16 million copies worldwide was probably a surprise to Reprise and to Green Day themselves, but it propelled them out of small venues into arenas and through the medium of MTV into the living rooms of American youth. Green Day were a breath of fresh air and, despite being depicted as bubblegum punk-rockers, their music, attitude and element of sheer fun resonated with new fans and fans of the original punk-rock bands alike. They could detect a similar spirit in these brash, young American pups who not only dyed their hair blue, green and peroxide blonde but seemed to enjoy being pelted by mud and grass at a reconstituted Woodstock Festival.

DOOKIE turned Green Day into millionaires, not bad going for three boys in their early twenties. Their success had its dark side, however. It sharpened the resentment felt towards them by their peers, and their gruelling schedule of gigs, promotions and awards ceremonies took its toll. There was also the pressure that their next album should live up to expectation. Fortunately, the spiky INSOMNIAC (1995) delivered musically, although the total worldwide sales forecast (in the region of 3.5 million units) was always going to be a struggle compared with DOOKIE'S huge success. Although subsequent albums like NIMROD (1997) and WARNING (2000) were not as commercially successful, they did generate vital singles like 'Good Riddance (Time Of Your Life)', 'Minority' and 'Warning', displaying the tenacity of the band as well as a more questing and expansive song-writing palette from Billie Joe Armstrong.

The abandonment of the CIGARETTES AND VALENTINES album in 2003 was a vital crossroads. That the band elected not to re-record the songs on the (allegedly) lost master tapes suggests that the direct back-to-basics material was not a direction that Green Day wished to pursue. The problem was that, at this stage, the band were unsure as to which path to follow. It was probably while recording as fake electro-rock band The Network that Green Day reconnected with each other and discovered anew the life-affirming fun that making music together had given them in their earlier days. This studio experimentation led to the track 'Homecoming', which in turn resulted in a full-blown punk-rock opera, perhaps one of the most startling and ambitious left turns any modern rock band has undertaken. The sentiment behind AMERICAN IDIOT (2004) saw Billie Joe Armstrong serve as a lightning rod for the American psyche. Not only did he question the war in Iraq, but also the established patterns of American political and cultural behaviour, asking where the average American fitted into this disparate jigsaw. AMERICAN IDIOT, musically and lyrically, was a tour-de-force. Along with Nirvana's NEVERMIND and The Sex Pistol's NEVER MIND THE BOLLOCKS..., it is one of the most influential rock albums released in the last 50 years.

The success of **AMERICAN IDIOT** propelled it, and the singles taken from it, up the charts around the world and gave the band a new fanbase that remains loyal today. Green Day became spokesmen for their generation, displaying in interviews and public appearances a seriousness and cultural awareness that had been glossed over in previous years. This newly revealed side to the band did much to dispel the more established view of them, which largely centred on their alleged pot smoking and championship displays of buffoonery. Green Day had become a force to be reckoned with, a band with something to say and the ability to connect with audiences ranging from 1,000 to 65,000.

Green Day now became something of a touring circus, complete with pyrotechnics, vast video screens and all manner of tour-memorabilia. Their performance was an exuberant mix of anthemic songs and audience participation: lucky fans were plucked from the crowd to join the band on stage and take over the helm of the Operation Ivy track 'Knowledge'. Fans would rehearse on guitar, bass and drums before attending a concert – some even bringing their own guitars and drumsticks – in the hope of being called up on stage. This wonderfully theatrical event related directly back to Green Day's punk roots at Gilman where the gap between audience and performers was overcome through rehearsal and attitude rather than competence.

The follow-up to **AMERICAN IDIOT** was another rock opera, **21ST CENTURY BREAKDOWN** (2009), which was snapped up by fans worldwide and was the subject of another sell-out world tour in 2009/2010. At this point, Green Day were rightfully considered the biggest rock band in the world. They were not only outselling artists such as U2, The Foo Fighters, Iron Maiden, Metallica, Radiohead, Kings Of Leon, the Killers and Coldplay, but were also being woven into the fabric of contemporary culture. This ranged from an appearance in **THE SIMPSONS MOVIE** (2007) to being only the second band ever (after The Beatles) to enjoy their own **ROCK BAND** video game. The cherry on the cake was the translation of **AMERICAN IDIOT** onto Broadway where it ran for over 450 appearances, a milestone that Pete Townshend's **TOMMY** and **QUADROPHENIA** never achieved. Saying that, the latter two were both made into feature films and there is a strong possibility that **AMERICAN IDIOT** will make it onto the cinema screen with Billie Joe Armstrong as one of the cast. Whether Tre Cool will get a part as memorable as Keith Moon's Uncle Ernie remains to be seen.

That there is talk of a film of **AMERICAN IDIOT** shows how far Green Day have come. **GREEN DAY REVEALED** celebrates their entire career to date, taking the reader in words and pictures from their early days as Sweet Children, their debut musical statement on Lookout! Records back in 1989 and hand-to-mouth tours playing living rooms, squats and small venues to the interstellar sales of **DOOKIE**, the temperate years and then back to the highs of commercial and critical success after **AMERICAN IDIOT** that they are still enjoying today.

Not bad going for a three-man punk band from Berkeley...

IAN SHIRLEY

IN THE BEGINNING. 1986-92.

1986—92

Although Green Day is now one of the biggest bands in the world, selling out stadiums from America to Australia, there would not have been a band had it not been for 924 Gilman Street. It was this legendary musical co-operative venue in Berkeley, California, that gave the aspirations of Billie Joe Armstrong and Michael Ryan Pritchard focus and a desire to translate from members of the audience to performers on the stage.

Once this ambition had been realized – assisted vitally by original drummer John Kiffmeyer – Green Day began to play wherever they could. They soon signed to small independent label Lookout! Records to record EPs and two full-length LPs. Early tours of America and Europe honed their musicianship, playing venues from squats to small punk venues. Tre Cool replaced the departing Kiffmeyer, and Green Day began to attract a growing number of fans.

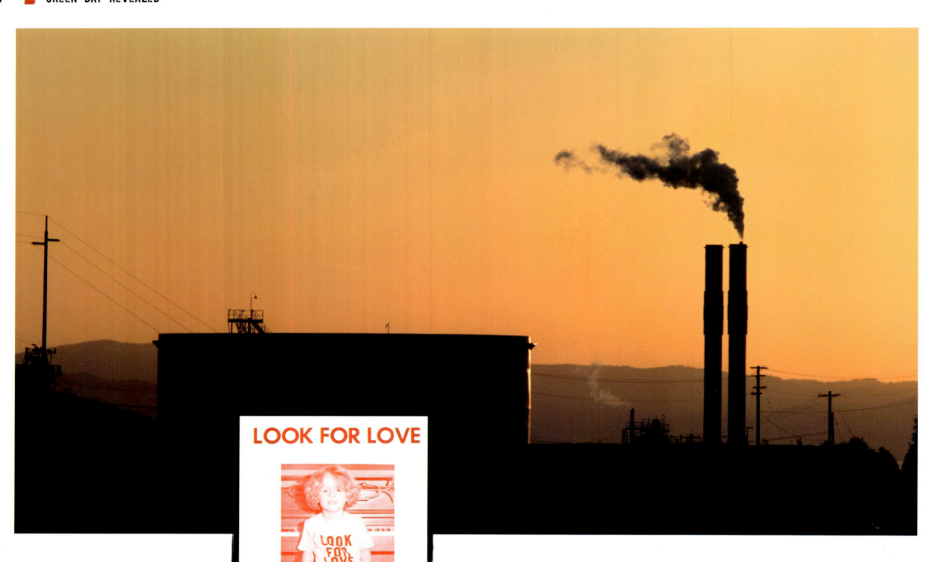

LOOK FOR LOVE

"Billie Joe"

Recorded by "Billie Joe" on Fiat Records

Pre-1986
GROWING UP

Billie Joe Armstrong was born on 17 February 1972 in the town of Rodeo in the San Francisco Bay Area. The town was dominated by a vast oil refinery and referred to as 'Bordeo' by the local youth. He was the youngest of six children and recorded 'Look For Love' aged five, released in a limited run of 800 by a local music store owner. Billie Joe's father died of cancer when he was 10, forcing his mother to work full time, and the children had to grow up fast. Music education continued at the hands of local musician George Cole on a Fernandes Stratocaster Billie loved so much he nicknamed it 'Blue' and later acquired it.

1986
SPRING: SWEET CHILDREN ARE BORN

Michael Ryan Pritchard (Mike Dirnt) was born on 4 May 1972 and given up for adoption by his mother when he was six weeks old. He grew up in El Sobrante, near Rodeo, and became Billie Joe's best friend. By their teens Dirnt and Billie Joe had formed a jamming band with another friend Sean Hughes, rotating drummers. They eventually settled on the name Sweet Children, inspired by one of Armstrong's early songs. Musically, they leant towards punk and grew tighter through rehearsal. They were joined by former Isocracy drummer John Kiffmeyer, a.k.a Al Sobrante (born 11 July 1969), whose drive and local musical connections gave them focus.

1987

APRIL: 924 GILMAN STREET

'Isn't it time we created a real alternative?'

Tim Yohannan was the driving force behind local radio show and then fanzine **MAXIMUMROCKNROLL** and it was his determination that led to the establishment of a new music venue in Berkeley at 924 Gilman Street. Run along co-operative lines with a no drugs, no alcohol and no major bands policy it opened its doors on 1 January 1987 and soon became the focus of the local music scene. It promoted hardcore and nu-punk music, staging gigs by a diverse number of artists including the Mr T Experience, Monsula, Isocracy and the undisputed darlings of the local scene, Operation Ivy.

APRIL: OPERATION IVY

'Everyone's got their band,' Billie Joe told **SPIN** in 2005, 'and I've got to say that Operation Ivy was definitely one that changed me.' With a line-up of Jesse Michaels (vocals), Tim Armstrong (guitar), Dave Mello (drums) and Matt Freeman (bass), Operation Ivy played their first gig together in April 1987 and their hedonistic mix of ska/punk won a devoted local audience at Gilman. Their debut EP **HECTIC** (1988) and LP **ENERGY** (1989) were both released on the local Lookout! label and, before the band split in 1989, Operation Ivy had even conducted a short club tour of America.

1989

SPRING: SIGN TO LOOKOUT! RECORDS

Sweet Children began to build a reputation as they had started to play at Gilman and at local parties. One night, they played at a house party in front of an audience of five, supporting The Lookouts, another local punk-rock outfit. Larry Livermore, who had formed the band and was playing that night, was also co-founder of Lookout! Records. Livermore liked Sweet Children's energy and conviction, and offered them the opportunity to record an EP. Lookout! had originally been formed with the sole purpose of releasing The Lookouts' records, but soon began documenting the emerging Bay Area punk scene as well as recording like-minded bands from other cities, including Screeching Weasel and The Queers. Strong sales of Operation Ivy's debut six-track **HECTIC** EP allowed Livermore's hand-to-mouth operation to fund Sweet Children's EP offer.

APRIL: '1,000 HOURS'

Recorded quickly and cheaply at the Art of Ears Studio in Hayward, California, Sweet Children's debut EP was laid down with a minimum of fuss and overdubs. '1,000 Hours', 'Dry Ice', 'Only Of You' and 'The One I Want' revealed a young band full of nu-punk attitude but, like The Buzzcocks and British Powerpop movement before them, with a compulsive melodic edge. Anarchy came in the form of an eleventh-hour name change with the EP released as Green Day. 'A Green Day is a day with lots of green bud where you just sit around taking bong hits,' Mike later told a fanzine.

MAY: GREEN DAY'S GILMAN DEBUT

As members of the local scene, Billie Joe and Mike fulfilled their ambition for Sweet Children to play Gilman on 24th November 1988. They were allowed to prop up a bill delivering a short, energetic set that included self-penned material and cover versions like The Who's 'My Generation' and Chuck Berry's 'Johnny B. Goode'. Their first gig at Gilman as Green Day took place on 28th May 1989 in the wake of the April release of their debut EP 1,000 HOURS. The headliners were Billie Joe's beloved Operation Ivy who – sadly – performed their final gig before splitting up.

1990

APRIL: 39/SMOOTH

Green Day's debut LP was recorded and mixed between 29 December 1989 and 2 January 1990 at Art of Ears Studio. Musically it was an affirmative affair, at odds with other bands on the Gilman scene, with energetic melodic hooks and lyrics ranging from teenage infatuation ('At The Library', 'Disappearing Boy') to the desire of children such as Billie Joe and Mike from difficult backgrounds to belong ('Road To Acceptance'). 'Hey, can you hear me?', Billie Joe sang on the pert track 'Rest' and, on 13 April, fans who bought the LP, on black, clear and green vinyl, could.

JUNE: FIRST US TOUR

Green Day's first 45-date tour was set up through contacts of Lookout! and the band's own endeavour. They headed into the great American unknown in Billie Joe's older brother's converted Ford Econoline van. Playing anywhere and everywhere from house parties to small punk venues for food, money and fuel, the band managed to get by, sleeping on floors, sofas and the occasional bed. At a gig in Minneapolis Billie Joe met 22-year-old Adrienne Nesser and, although she had a boyfriend and he had a girlfriend, there was a connection that led to correspondence and increasingly longer and longer telephone calls.

AUTUMN: DRUMMER DIFFICULTIES

Despite a US tour and debut LP under their belt, Green Day were living hand-to-mouth. It was with an eye upon his future that the older John Kiffmeyer decided to enrol at Humboldt State College in Arcata, California, 250 miles north of the Bay Area. If he expected the band to adapt to his study schedule he was wrong. Although Kiffmeyer played some gigs, Dave 'E.C.' Henwood from Filth and The Wynona Ryders initially warmed the drum stool and it was not long before Billie Joe and Mike found a permanent solution in a local player on the Gilman scene from Larry Livermore's band The Lookouts: Tre Cool.

NOVEMBER: TRE'S FIRST GIG

Born 9 December 1972, Frank Edwin Wright was raised in the mountainous area of Mendocino where, as a 12-year-old pre-teen, he started playing in Larry Livermore's Lookouts. Like the drummer Dee Generate in British band Eater, his energy and enthusiasm made up for a lack of technique which was swiftly acquired as The Lookouts began playing around their local area and a few years later at Gilman. Livermore gave Wright the nickname Tre Cool – unflappable, excitable – and he slipped into the role of drummer, pot smoker and king of Green Day mischief like a hand into a leather glove.

1991

JANUARY: GREEN DAY TOUR WITH TRE COOL

Tre Cool's full-time occupation of the Green Day drum-stool began with a period of transition. During this time Kiffmeyer would occasionally play, even turning up at gigs where Tre played but, by late 1991, Cool was the band's official drummer. They began playing any dates the band could grab, in the Bay Area and around America. The same age as Billie Joe and Mike Dirnt, Cool was the missing piece in the musical jigsaw. His arrival heralded a new era for the band which, as a result, grew tighter as a live unit. The trio were able to share the hardships and small pleasures of being a young band with a growing reputation.

1992

JANUARY: KERPLUNK

Green Day returned to the Art Of Ears Studio in May and September 1991 to lay down tracks for their second LP **KERPLUNK**. Produced by Andy Ernst and the band themselves for $1,500, the 12 tracks were brash, confident and compulsive. As a songwriter, Billie Joe showed a maturity far beyond his tender years on relationship songs such as 'One For The Razorbacks', 'Words I May Have Ate' and '2,000 Light Years Away', whilst the chemistry and interplay of the trio was rock solid on 'Welcome To Paradise' and 'Christie Road'. Tre Cool's countrified 'Dominated Love Slave' showed a wicked sense of humour.

JANUARY: '2,000 LIGHT YEARS AWAY'

Phone calls, letters and the physical distance that separated them was to eventually draw Billie Joe and Adrienne together as a couple. His feelings and emotions were pertly expressed on the track '2,000 Light Years Away' which was a sweet love song armoured in guitar chords. 'I hold my breath and close my eyes and dream about her,' sang Billie Joe, revealing a sensitive side that, as well as appealing to Adrienne, attracted a growing number of female fans who had begun to attend Green Day gigs. Green Day began to sell out small clubs due to fanzine coverage and word of mouth.

WINTER: OUTGROWING THE LABEL

KERPLUNK sold 10,000 copies on its first day of release, a phenomenal amount for a band on a small independent label in the Bay Area. Green Day's work ethic and compelling live performances began to ram small American venues although, due to Lookouts' limited nationwide distribution, some fans could not get their hands on the album. The band also funded a trip to Europe where they ended up playing 64 dates in three months from clubs to squats, even staging an impromptu pre-launch party for KERPLUNK in Southampton, England on 17th December 1991 when they received finished copies via courier.

HITTING THE BIG TIME: 1993-97

1993-97

The success of Nirvana's 'Smells Like Teen Spirit' and NEVERMIND (1991) steamrolling around the world in 1992 alerted major labels to the potential of independent rock music. With two albums and a growing armada of fans, Green Day were seen as an act with similar potential. Their major label debut, DOOKIE (1994), fulfilled this potential, racking up phenomenal international sales of an estimated 16 million copies. Laced with hit singles, including 'Longview' and 'Basket Case', DOOKIE propelled the band from small venues to arena tours.

Green Day also experienced a backlash from the punk scene that had nurtured them, with accusations that they were selling out and abandoning the DIY and co-operative principles of the movement. Although this wounded a band trying to come to terms with commercial and financial success, their live reputation and a visually memorable Woodstock appearance delivered them an international army of fans.

1993

SPRING: GREEN DAY LEAVE LOOKOUT!

Despite their love of pot and good times, Green Day took their music seriously and handed over the day-to-day running of their affairs to Elliot Cahn and Jeff Saltzman of Cahn-Man Management whose track record included The Melvins and Mudhoney. The first item upon an agreed agenda was to upgrade their record label. Despite their punk credentials and lifestyle, Green Day could clearly see the benefits of signing to a major label which could not only distribute their records properly across America, but also reach countries like Britain and Germany into which their recent tour confirmed Lookout! had no penetration.

SPRING: LABELS PITCH FOR GREEN DAY

With Green Day's first two LPs selling 30,000 copies each, and mindful of the breakthrough for independent rock made by Nirvana, several A&R men made the pilgrimage to Green Day's bunker on 2243 Ashby Street. Geffen took Green Day to see Nirvana play live and even paid for them to go to Disneyland as part of a failed courtship. Former guitarist and Reprise A&R man Rob Cavallo, producer of The Muffs' major label debut, also made the trip to Ashby, witnessing new material like 'Longview'. He ended up getting stoned with Billie Joe, Mike and Tre after an informal jam session.

APRIL: SIGN WITH REPRISE

With its long association with Frank Sinatra, Reprise was, on first inspection, hardly a label that appeared to suit Green Day, who signed up for a five-album deal. Then again, Reprise had signed Jimi Hendrix in the 1960s and, as a subsidiary of Warner Brothers, had access to an effective promotional and marketing machine that extended around the world. Warner had also signed R.E.M. in 1988 and The Flaming Lips in 1992, showing that this major label was prepared to invest in and back independent music and take it – without artistic compromise – into the mainstream.

OCTOBER: TOUR WITH BAD RELIGION

In October, Green Day headed out on tour, supporting Bad Religion. For Green Day, playing alongside this long-established band (who formed in 1979) was a perfect fit. They had moved from an independent to a major label in 1993 – Epitaph to Atlantic – but also tapped into a similar punk demographic as Green Day, especially after scoring sub-mainstream success with RECIPE FOR HATE (1993). Armoured by long touring, Green Day's power, energy, stagecraft, enthusiasm and melodic appeal served notice that they were the Next-Big-Thing-In-Waiting, even if they were travelling to gigs in a converted Bookmobile complete with TV, VCR and stereo equipment.

WINTER: THE BACKLASH

'Punk died the day The Clash signed to CBS,' the editor of famed punk fanzine SNIFFIN' GLUE stated back in 1977 and similar sentiments were expressed in Bay Area fanzines in 1993 after Green Day's Reprise deal. By moving from a label with limited distribution to one with worldwide reach, they were seen as betraying the collective independent principles the new American punk movement had inherited from the original UK explosion. That Green Day had spent two years living hand-to-mouth appeared to count for nothing. 'We sell out every show we play,' Tre later told MELODY MAKER.

WINTER: FOCUSING ON THE MUSIC

Green Day had already worked new material like 'Longview' and 'Burnout' into their set lists in 1993 and 'Basket Case' was on demos sent out to record companies. KERPLUNK'S 'Welcome To Paradise' was also earmarked for re-recording on their major label debut. 'I had just got thrown out of my house when I was 17 and ended up in this warehouse with 14 other people,' Billie Joe told NME in 1994 about this song's genesis. 'There were artists and freaks and junkies, bums and punks, all through that neighbourhood and that was a big part of my growing up.'

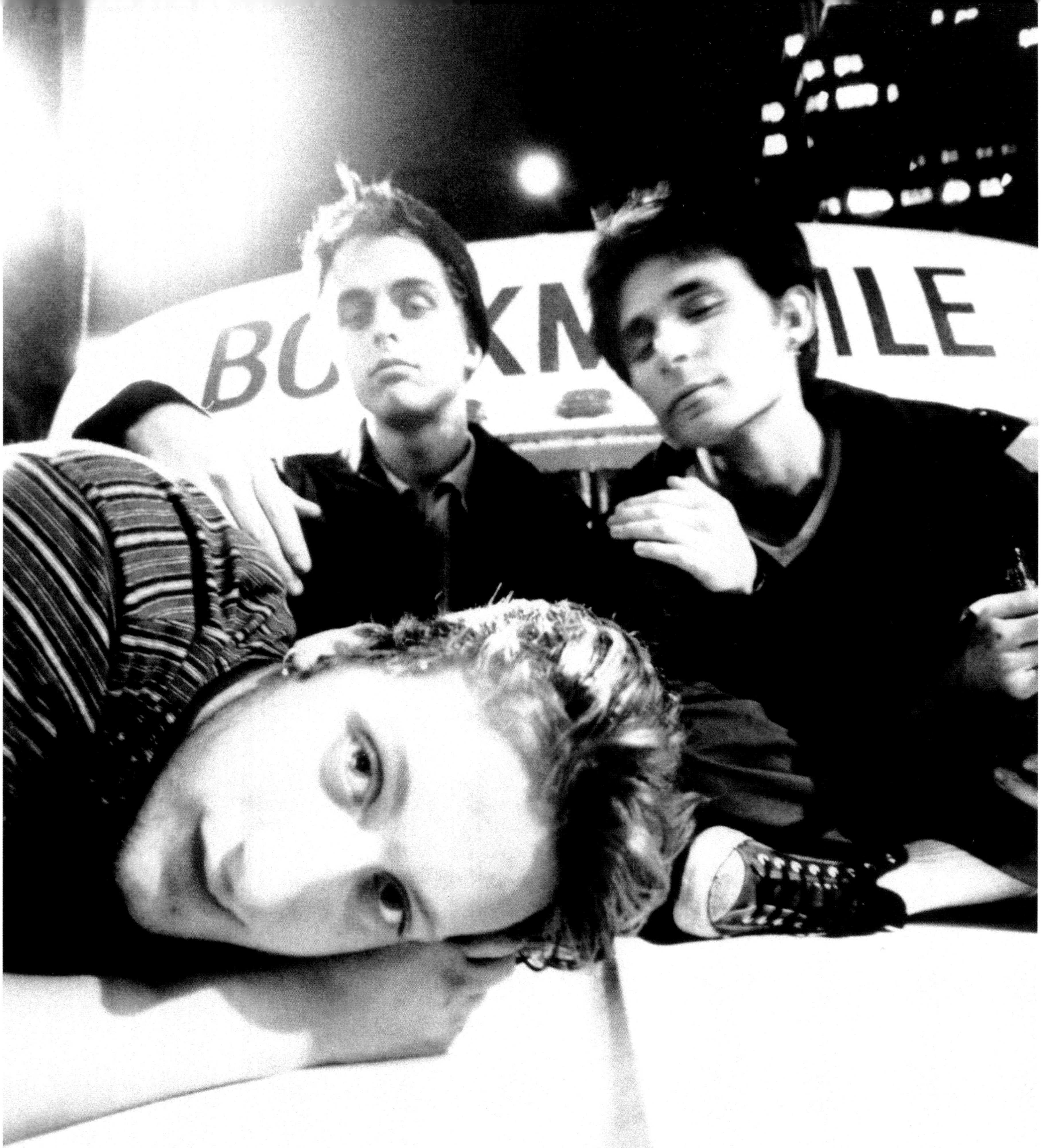

1994

JANUARY: THE BOOKMOBILE AND EUROPEAN TOUR

'It was a travelling library that was found in Phoenix, Arizona, and converted into an RV [recreation vehicle],' Billie Joe told a TV interviewer in 1994 when discussing the Bookmobile inside the vehicle. 'A lot of people come up to us and say, "Do you have books for sale in there?". We don't even read.' The converted Bookmobile was Green Day's home for American tours and a vast improvement on the cramped Econoline van previously deployed. 'Tre Cool's dad is the driver/spiritual leader,' continued Billie Joe, who slept on a futon. 'Drummer producer!' chipped in Mike beside him. Of course, when the band returned to Europe for more dates the Bookmobile stayed at home.

JANUARY: FUNDRAISING

HIV/AIDS caused death and heartbreak amongst the gay community in the San Francisco Bay Area and so was an issue that Green Day and the general punk community was aware of. In 1992, HIV/AIDS sufferer Bob Caviano founded the charity LIFEbeat to work with musicians and the music industry to educate young people about HIV/AIDS prevention. In January 1994, Green Day undertook a promotional signing session at a New York record store to raise money for the charity and, in typical fashion, adorned the collecting buckets with encouraging graffiti messages, such as 'donate or die' and 'donate you f***ers.'

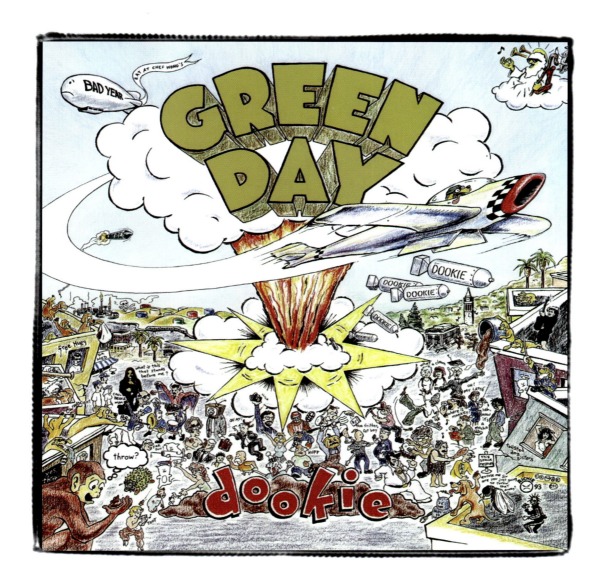

FEBRUARY: DOOKIE

Rob Cavallo was given the responsibility of producing Green Day's major label debut. Fears that life would be sucked out of their material by over-production were unfounded. 'You've got a bigger studio, better equipment,' Mike Dirnt told a fanzine scribe. 'The whole album sounds bigger.' The resulting tracks were powerful, energetic and vibrant. Lyrically, Billie Joe reviewed masturbation ('Coming Clean'): 'I found out what it takes to be a man'; boredom ('Longview'): 'change the channels for an hour or two'; and broken relationships ('In The End'): 'how long will he last before he's a creep in the past.'

FEBRUARY: THE DOOKIE COVER STORY

Green Day chose local artist and former bass player for The Wynona Riders, Richie Bucher to illustrate their cover based on their album title: DOOKIE. The resulting picture resembled something out of the fevered mind of 1960s Freak Brothers' artist Gilbert Shelton. It featured dogs in a jet aeroplane and on various rooftops dropping and throwing excrement onto a cavalcade below which consisted of an array of characters ranging from a caveman, Elvis (or an impersonator) to what looks like Angus from AC/DC, as well as a hungry fly asking a dog about to throw a turd, 'Excuse me sir, are you just going to throw that away?'.

FEBRUARY: 'LONGVIEW'

The first single culled from **DOOKIE** was 'Longview' which, with its stalking, melodic bass-line and guitar assault chorus offsetting this tale of boredom and masturbation, was a perfect primer for the album. The necessary promotional video was shot at the band's Ashby Street habitat and segued between shots of Billie Joe singing as he watched TV to the band playing in cramped conditions where Billie Joe looked like a young Joe Strummer. The compelling strength of the song and Warner's strong marketing arm soon saw 'Longview' begin to be rotated on MTV, which helped sell the single.

SUMMER: TOUR WITH PANSY DIVISION

Rather than pull up the drawbridge and dismiss their past, Green Day allocated the support slot on their first Reprise-backed US tour to Lookout! band Pansy Division. This openly gay act opened for Green Day during 28 pre-**DOOKIE** dates in July at venues that generally held 1,000 people and post-**DOOKIE** dates culminating in the two bands playing 15,000-seat arenas and Madison Square Garden. 'I got to see first-hand what happens to a band that goes from nothing to selling 14 million albums in one year,' Pansy bassist Chris Freeman told the *Santa Cruz Good Times*.

SUMMER: KEEPING THEIR FANS

Sales of **DOOKIE** began to exceed the wildest dreams of Reprise and even Tre Cool – whose dreams were pretty wild – which meant that a tour that began in mid-sized venues would end with the band playing arenas. Gigs were sold out as Green Day stipulated that ticket prices remain low, sometimes just $5. 'We lost a lot of money. We basically paid for it out of our own pocket,' Mike Dirnt told one fanzine. 'We're still not making anything. We've lost thousands of dollars on this tour. Something like $15,000. Doesn't sound like a lot, whatever, but I guess it is.'

JULY: GREEN DAY GET MARRIED

'I was really nervous so I started pounding beers,' Billie Joe told **ROLLING STONE** in January 1995 about his wedding day, 'and so did Adrienne.' The ceremony on 2 July, which mixed the best vows from Catholic, Protestant and Jewish religious franchises, lasted five minutes, allowing friends, family and band mates to carry on pounding beers in the backyard where the ceremony was held. 'Then we went to the Claremont Hotel,' added Billie Joe, 'and f***ed like bunnies.' Tre Cool later tied the knot with his girlfriend Lisea Lyons in March 1995 and Mike married in 1996.

JULY: JOIN THE LOLLAPALOOZA TOUR

The concept of the Lollapalooza touring festival was established in 1991 as a farewell for Jane's Addiction supported by artists across musical genres, like rapper Ice T. The revitalization of alternative rock made Lollapalooza an annual affair. Green Day were added to the opening line-up for July and August dates, and the trio experienced the unusual sensation of performing in early afternoon daylight to audiences still arriving or getting a good place to watch The Smashing Pumpkins later in the day. 'Why DOOKiE?' a female MTV interviewer asked the boys backstage. 'It comes out of your arse,' replied green-haired Tre.

AUGUST: WOODSTOCK

If the original Woodstock was all about peace and mud, the second, 25 years later, was all about mud and Green Day. The band were pelted with what looked like half a field, with 'Green Lanterns' extended to eight minutes by Tre and Mike as Billie Joe told the hostile audience, 'I'm not going to become a mud hippie like you,' attempted a singalong and threw mud and grass back. With the show going out live, Green Day's sportsmanship in the face of adversity was the festival highlight. Mike Dirnt lost a tooth after being mistaken for a stage invader by security.

SEPTEMBER: RIOT AT THE HATCH SHELL

Local Boston radio station WFNX had pre-arranged for Green Day to play a free concert on 9 September, but **DOOKIE** sales and interest generated by the Woodstock mud fight saw an estimated 100,000 overwhelm organizers and police who expected no more than 20,000. As the band performed, the audience surged forward causing the lighting rig to swing enough for organizers to stop the show as Green Day played their seventh song, 'F.O.D.'. 'It was a complete riot!' Tre later told the **NME**, but Green Day enjoyed giving autographs to 15 inmates from a local prison assisting security as part of their rehabilitation!

OCTOBER: 'WELCOME TO PARADISE'

The rotation of first single 'Longview' on MTV and radio helped establish Green Day in the living rooms of America, as did the exciting, live performance promo of the second single taken from **DOOKIE**, 'Welcome To Paradise'. Originally, this track had been on **KERPLUNK** and was re-recorded for **DOOKIE** as the band had only written it a week before recording **KERPLUNK** and wanted to give what had become a strong song in their live sets much more power. 'We just wanted to show it as a solid song, and we thought it fit better with this album too,' said Mike.

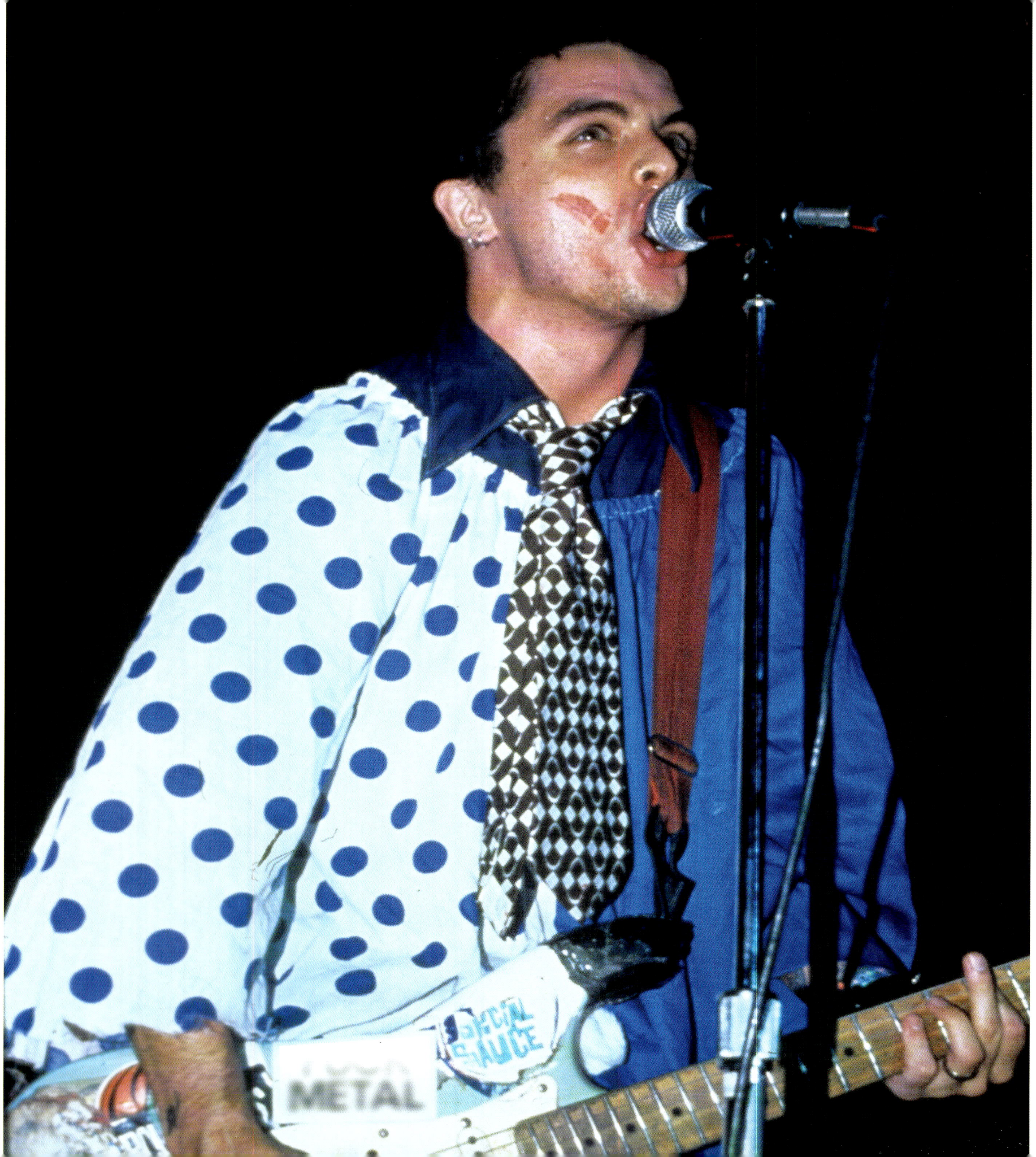
METAL

NOVEMBER: 'BASKET CASE'

Opening with the famous line 'Do you have the time/to listen to me whine?', 'Basket Case' was the third single from DOOKIE and remains one of Green Day's best-loved songs. Although the lyrics deal with the serious subject of Billie Joe's anxiety attacks: 'I think I'm cracking up', the panache of the song helped break the band Stateside, reach the Top 10 in the UK and chart heavily in other European countries. Aptly, the promotional video was filmed – at the band's request – inside a California mental asylum, with Green Day chirpily performing the song as 'musical therapy.'

DECEMBER: APPEARANCE ON THE LATE SHOW

As well as playing live shows, Green Day undertook a wide range of promotional activities from press interviews to showcasing singles and DOOKIE on American nationwide TV. The shows they appeared on ranged from LATE NIGHT WITH CONAN O'BRIEN, where they performed 'Welcome To Paradise', to the LATE SHOW WITH DAVID LETTERMAN where they played 'Basket Case'. Both O'Brien and Letterman waved copies of DOOKIE at the camera during their introductions as a perfect piece of product placement and although Rosanne Barr did not do the same on SATURDAY NIGHT LIVE the band performed two songs, 'When I Come Around' and 'Geek Stink Breath'.

DECEMBER: MADISON SQUARE GARDEN

'We've been on tour since February and this is our last show today,' announced Billie Joe to screaming fans at Madison Square Garden on 5 December. The band then went on to perform a cover version of Operation Ivy's 'Knowledge' that had been part of their set throughout a gruelling schedule that had taken them around America and Europe on an ever-growing wave of **DOOKIE** mania. Billie Joe, like Iggy Pop, was getting a reputation for exposing his bare buttocks and celebrated freedom from touring at the end of the show by performing 'She' naked with only his low-slung treasured 'Blue' guitar covering his modesty.

DECEMBER: EXHAUSTION HITS

Musically, Green Day were a breath of fresh air to the music press in both America and the UK who, as well as running a copious number of features on the band, portrayed Green Day as the spearhead of a new wave of punk bands. 'We've made people feel good about the fact that they're lonely, loser nerds – ugly, fat, skinny, *anything,*' Tre proudly told the **NME**. Speaking of anything, the band turned down a guest appearance on **SESAME STREET** and by the end of 1994 were exhausted, 'mentally, you start slipping down the shithole,' Billie Joe stated in the same interview.

1995

SPRING: THE GREEN DAY FAMILY GROWS

Billie Joe and Adrienne discovered the morning after their wedding – 3 July 1994 – that she was pregnant and their first child, Joseph, was born in February 1995. A second son, Joshua, was born in September 1998. Tre Cool's daughter was born in January 1995 and he married Lisea Lyons in March, although subsequently they divorced. He remarried in 2000, siring a son before again divorcing. Mike Dirnt married in 1996 and his daughter was born in 1997, although he later divorced his first wife. Happily, he remarried in 2009 and he and his wife have a son and another daughter.

MARCH: GRAMMY WINNERS

The icing was applied to the cake in 1995 when DOOKIE won a Grammy for Best Alternative Music Performance, easily beating off competition from Tori Amos, The Crash Test Dummies, Sarah McLachlan and Nine Inch Nails. Although the band won no MTV awards, 'Longview' had been nominated for Best Group Video in 1994 and 'Basket Case' was nominated in 1995, showing how far the band had come in 12 months. Mike and Tre won outstanding bassist and outstanding drummer respectively at the more low-key Bammys – Bay Area Music Awards – hosted by BAM (Bay Area Music) magazine. Carlos Santana won Best Guitarist....

SUMMER: MONEY, MONEY, MONEY

The success of **DOOKIE** made Green Day millionaires. Money became a sensitive subject in interviews as their wealth and success made them an even greater target for the Green Day = sellout brigade, 'but if anyone says anything, I just run them over in my Ferrari,' joked Tre, deflecting *yet* another question on the subject. The band made a charitable donation in the region of $40,000 to Food Not Bombs in San Francisco that fed the homeless, '...fed my ass a couple of times a few years back,' said Billie Joe, 'it's good to put something back into our community.'

SUMMER: MOVING FORWARD

'The f***ed up thing about being famous and having money,' Billie Joe told **SPiN** magazine, 'is that if you complain about something, people are like "what the f*** are *you* complaining about? You don't have to worry about money or a place to live." I feel I don't have anyone to vent my frustrations to because they won't understand.' This sense of dislocation and alienation from old friends, associates and even family informed many of the new songs that Billie Joe began to write and rehearse with the band as they prepared to record their eagerly awaited follow-up to **DOOKIE**.

JULY: TAKING CONTROL

'We were going in one direction, they were going in another,' Billie Joe told **NME** when discussing Green Day's uncoupling from their management deal with Elliot Cahn and Jeff Saltzman. 'There was no big fall out. They weren't trying to get us to do anything that we didn't want to do. It's just that no one on this earth knows what's best for us better than we do.' Cahn and Saltzman were probably concentrating upon (510) Records, a division of MCA which signed punk-rock bands China Drum and The Dance Hall Crashers (which included two former members of Operation Ivy).

SPECIAL DOUBLE ISSUE

Rolling Stone

ISSUE 724/725 • DECEMBER 28, 1995-JANUARY 11, 1996 • $3.95 • CAN $4.50

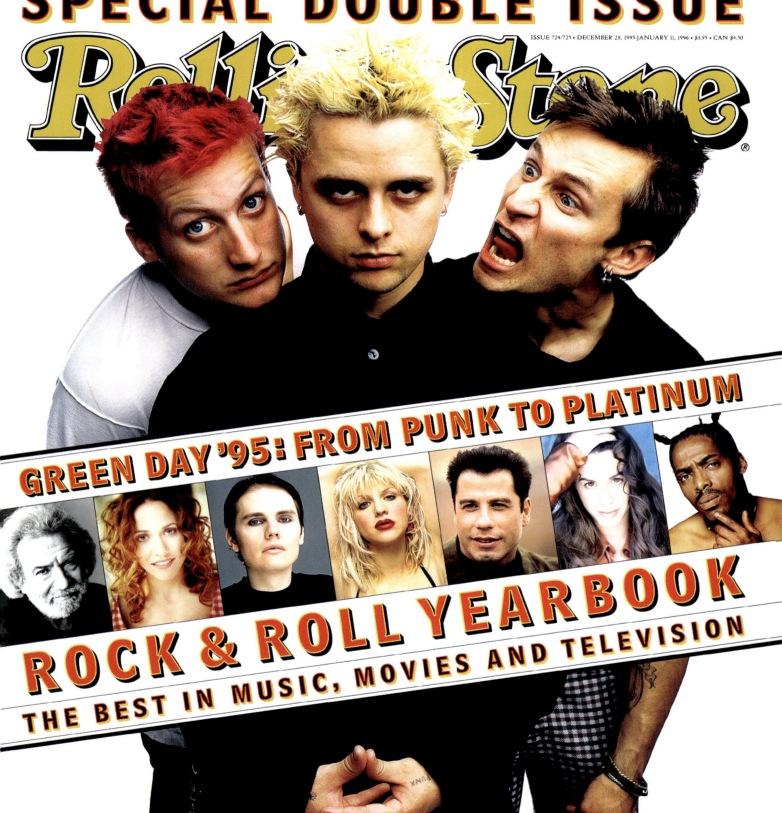

GREEN DAY '95: FROM PUNK TO PLATINUM

ROCK & ROLL YEARBOOK
THE BEST IN MUSIC, MOVIES AND TELEVISION

SEPTEMBER: 'GEEK STINK BREATH' VIDEO

The first single released from the eagerly awaited follow-up to
DOOKIE was 'Geek Stink Breath' where Billie Joe addressed the
side-effects of high amphetamine abuse, showing that Green Day
had no intention of peddling pop-fodder. The video showcased
the band performing the song intercut with scenes of a young
man receiving intense dental treatment. Green Day paid more
punk-rock dues by including a cover version of Berkeley punk
band Fang's 'I Wanna Be On TV' on the single, which included
the lyric 'gonna take off my pants', a command that Billie Joe
took to heart at Madison Square Garden – and beyond.

OCTOBER: INSOMNIAC

'We're hoping to scare a few people off with this,' Mike Dirnt told **NME** shortly before the band's fourth album was released. 'I swear to God I wouldn't mind cutting it down to one quarter of the audience we have.' With two band members losing sleep taming infants, **INSOMNIAC** was an apt title. Like Nirvana's **IN UTERO**, **INSOMNIAC** was never going to match both the expectation and sales of its predecessor. This was a driving, questing album and although it spawned no monster hits, 'Stuck With Me', the febrile 'Panic Song' and 'Walking Contradiction' showed that Green Day's fire had not been doused.

OCTOBER: INSOMNIAC COVER

As with **DOOKIE**, the band exercised their right to commission the cover art. They chose Winston Smith whose eye-catching, colourful collage and montage work for the seminal Dead Kennedys between 1980 and 1987 and also Alternative Tentacles had made him well known in American punk circles. The title of the **INSOMNIAC** illustration 'God told me to skin you alive' was taken from the Dead Kennedys' song 'I Kill Children' and, apart from their name, the only reference to Green Day in the eye-catching cover was in the detail of the girl on the cover holding Billie Joe's beloved guitar 'Blue.'

OCTOBER: '86'

The backlash that Green Day endured at the hands of the tight-knit, independent community based around Gilman only intensified when the band enjoyed success. The track '86' was Billie Joe's own spiteful rejoinder to a friend who asked him what he was doing back in the old neighbourhood and old haunts, saying to him, 'Did you lose something the last time you were here?'. At a time when the band needed to touch base with old friends and their punk past, that it was denied to them was something of a slap in the face. So Billie Joe slapped back.

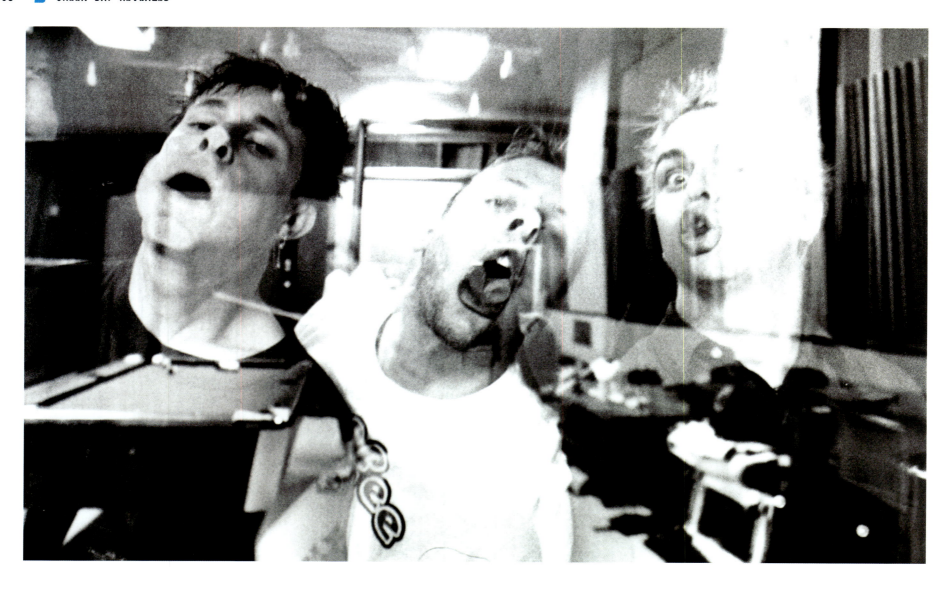

NOVEMBER: BILLIE JOE ARRESTED

Whenever Billie Joe felt Green Day were delivering a mediocre show he would take off his clothes, play naked or drop his trousers to show his buttocks to the audience. This would not only get a reaction from the crowd but also the band, thereby taking the performance to a new level. When they were a small club band, this worked to good effect but when the INSOMNIAC tour rolled into the Mecca Auditorium in Milwaukee on 21 November, police took exception to Billie Joe's bottom and arrested him after Green Day's hour-long set. Billie Joe was cited for 'indecent exposure' and had to pay bail of $141.85.

1996

JANUARY: INSOMNIAC GOES PLATINUM

'Every once in a while I have to say "F***, we're the biggest punk band in America right now",' Billie Joe told ROLLING STONE in their December 1995/January 1996 special double-issue. When it was released in 1995, INSOMNIAC debuted at No. 2 in the US charts and although it quickly sold two million copies and went double platinum, it was never going to be another DOOKIE. Ironically, in the UK the album reached No. 8 whereas DOOKIE had only got to No. 13; DOOKIE had remained in the UK charts for 91 weeks whilst INSOMNIAC only enjoyed a five-week run.

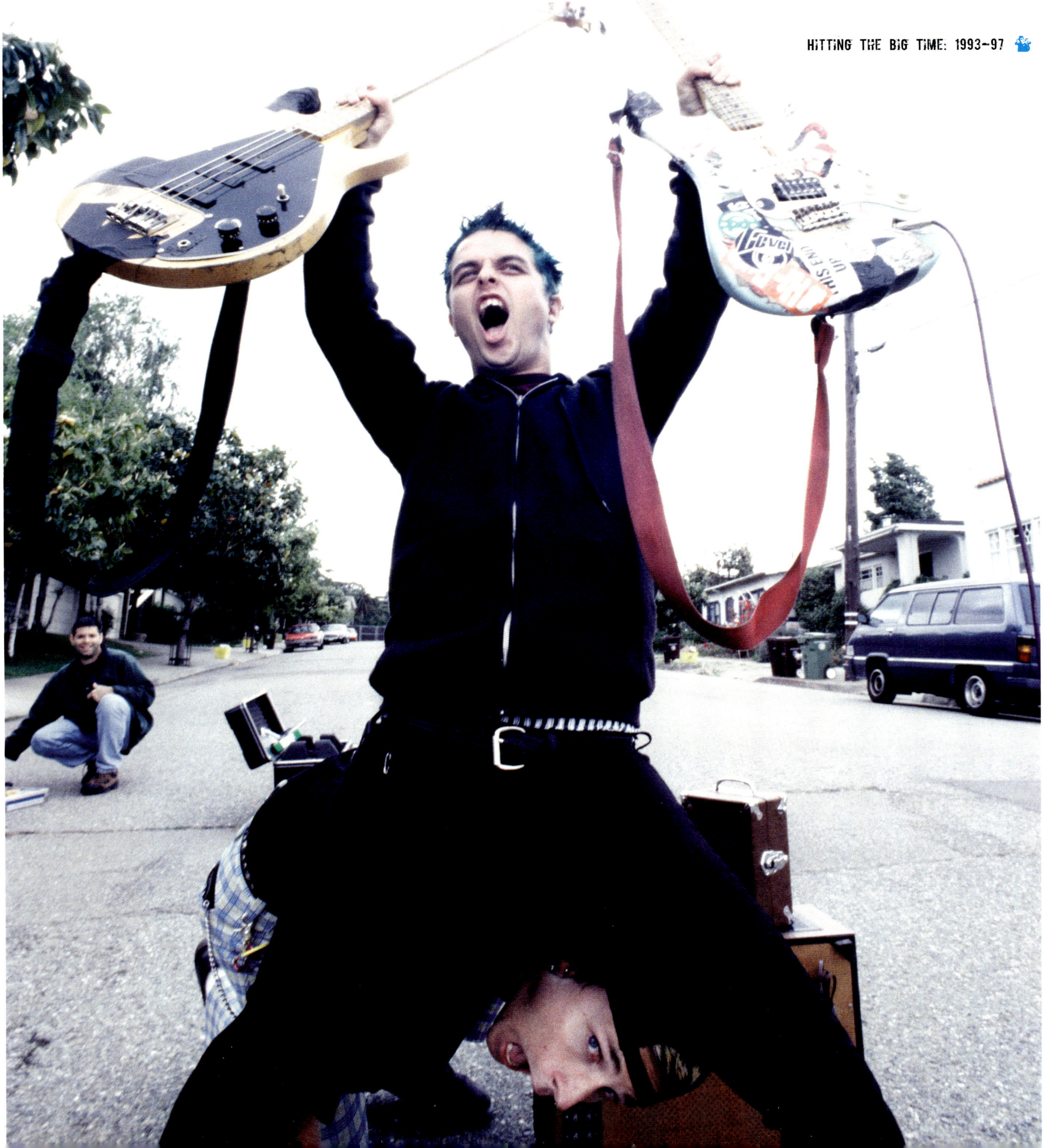

SPRING: INSOMNIAC TOUR

'On tour we have the most exciting lives in the world for one hour a day,' Mike Dirnt told **ROLLING STONE**, 'and the rest of the time it's the most boring job in the world.' When promoting **INSOMNIAC** on the road, Green Day were already displaying signs of rock battle-fatigue on a handful of American dates in December 1995 and January 1996. Although the general American public had first discovered them with **DOOKIE**, Green Day had been touring almost non-stop since 1992 and after the exhilarating roller-coaster ride of 1994 and 1995 they were close to running on empty.

JULY: 'BRAIN STEW'

'Brain Stew' was the second single taken from **INSOMNIAC** and concerns insomnia and isolation with lyrics like 'I'm counting sheep but running out'. This slow song, dominated by Billie Joe's chugging guitar, catapulted into warp-speed halfway through as it segued into 'Jaded'. This live mash-up was given lush video treatment by director Kevin Kerslake, with the first part shot in a rubbish tip in washed-out colour whilst the second part showcased the band storming away in a rehearsal space. It was a massive American radio hit, boosting sales of **INSOMNIAC** and perking up MTV rotation schedules.

WINTER: FEELING THE STRAIN

In retrospect, reading through press interviews given to the American, European and UK media prior to and after the release of **INSOMNIAC**, it is obvious today that the band were burnt out by five years of constant touring, with Billie Joe and Tre also having to juggle the responsibilities of being newlyweds and fathers of young children. 'I'm infertile!' Mike told **NME** in England as his fellow band members swapped nappy changing tips. With all three coming from unstable backgrounds, it was obvious that, as well as their music, Billie Joe and Tre took their paternal roles very seriously.

WINTER: EUROPEAN TOUR CANCELLATION

After completing the American leg of the **INSOMNIAC** tour, Green Day cancelled scheduled dates in Europe, giving 'exhaustion' as the honest reason for pulling out of the gigs. 'We were exhausted, wrecked, absolutely wrecked... We didn't know any more who we were, where we were. We just wanted to go home.' Billie Joe told **NEW YORK ROCK**. With money in the bank, they were able to relax for the first time in years, 'Out of everything that happened to me last year,' Billie Joe told **NME**, 'the most realistic thing was getting married and having a child. It puts everything in perspective.'

1997

SPRING: RETURNING TO THE STUDIO

The break from touring allowed Green Day to recharge their batteries, although with Billie Joe always writing songs they had a wealth of material to record when they returned to the studio in early 1997. During discussions with producer Rob Cavallo, the band stressed that they wanted to do something different musically. As sessions got underway, as well as high-octane rock there was an element of The Clash's LONDON CALLING in the air, with musical experimentation and even additional instrumentation, including horns on 'King For A Day' and a violin on 'Hitchin' A Ride' and 'Last Ride In'.

MARCH: THE BALCONY INCIDENT

The amazing thing about one of the most notorious Green Day incidents is that Tre Cool was not involved. On the evening of 23 March 1997, as Juliette Binoche was collecting an Oscar for Best Supporting Actress in THE ENGLISH PATIENT, Mike Dirnt made his own awards' contribution through clenched buttocks, depositing grown-up Dookie from his hotel-room balcony down onto hers. Binoche was not amused.

SPRING: MANAGEMENT IS HIRED

Managing themselves had allowed Green Day to make decisions like the cancellation of their European tour easily but it was impossible for them to handle the day-to-day running of a major band. Therefore, early in 1997 they turned to Pat Magnarella to oversee their affairs. Magnarella had started his career booking tours for alternative bands and moved on to managing the trajectory of artists like The BoDeans, The Goo Goo Dolls and Weezer in conjunction with Bob Cavallo (who is Rob Cavallo's father). This team jumped at the chance to handle the affairs of Green Day.

AUTUMN: TOWER RECORDS SIGNING

To launch NIMROD, Green Day performed a 40-minute set at Tower Records' flagship store in New York. Although 500 fans enjoyed the performance, Billie Joe exhorted the audience to start a riot ''cause you're not at Tower Records, you're at a Green Day concert.' Acting out the lyrics of The Clash song 'White Riot', the band proceeded to cause a riot of their own pouring beer and knocking over CD racks, and Billie Joe even spray painted 'f***' and 'Green Day' on the main window after mooning those outside. The post-gig signing was cancelled.

OCTOBER: NIMROD

NIMROD was a transitional album where Green Day began writing themselves out of the power pop-punk corner. Whilst 'The Grouch' and 'Platypus (I Hate You)' were staple Green Day fare, 'Redundant' was a dominant powerful rock song that contained amazingly frank lyrics: 'prototypes of what we were.' 'King For A Day' saw the band stumbling into ska territory and the instrumental 'Last Ride In' married a Duane Eddy-esque guitar melody to a vista of sound from xylophones to brass flourishes. The simple acoustic guitar, vocals and strings of 'Good Riddance (Time Of Your Life)' was the solid gold nugget.

WINTER: BEGINNING A TOUR RITUAL

Green Day went on the road to promote **NIMROD** with a total of 100 dates in America, Germany, the UK, Italy, Japan, Australia and South America. Although venues were smaller than in the **DOOKIE** days – a capacity between 1,000 and 3,000 people – the band had lost none of its ability to deliver great shows. It was on this tour that they began the ritual of inviting members of the audience – 'we need *three* volunteers' – onto the stage to take their place and enjoy the punk thrill of performing the Operation Ivy song 'Knowledge' watched by their heroes.

WINTER: ADELINE RECORDS

Named after the street that runs between Oakland and Berkeley, Adeline Records was founded in 1997 by Billie Joe, his wife Adrienne and skateboarder Jim Thiebaud. Adeline's first release was One Man Army's album **DEAD END STORIES** (1998) and the label soon established a roster of punk bands like Pinhead Gunpowder. They also represent Australian punk rockabilly trio The Living End who broke America with second album **ROLL ON** (2000). Adeline has released records by The Frustrators and the Network and has the rights to release Green Day albums on vinyl and – music aside – maintain a thriving clothing line.

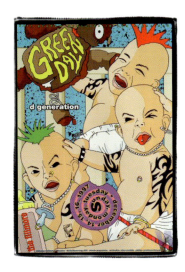

DECEMBER: FIGHT AT THE FILLMORE

Green Day had a hard-won reputation for delivering a good time: shows were littered with stage divers and the band usually enjoyed good relations with their fans. During a December date at the Fillmore, San Francisco, Billie Joe took exception to a heckler and called him out: 'I'll fight you right now, get up on the stage.' Seconds later, Billie Joe removed his guitar and jumped feet first into the audience, who screamed with delight. Finally, pulled out by security, Billie Joe yelled, 'just because we're rock stars doesn't mean we won't beat the living s*** out of you.'

DECLINE IN POPULARITY: 1998-2003

1998-2003

Although INSOMNIAC had failed to repeat the commercial success of DOOKIE, it had maintained Green Day's international momentum. Their constant touring had worn out their mental joints, leading to the cancellation of European dates in 1996; a period of reflection and musical re-evaluation followed.

The gap between NIMROD (1997) and WARNING (2000) removed Green Day from public eye and, coupled with musical experimentation, saw tours being booked into smaller venues. Green Day still performed with their customary energy and enthusiasm, but it was before a diminished but loyal fanbase. Despite the appearance of the evergreen single 'Good Riddance (Time Of Your Life)', the release of compilation album INTERNATIONAL SUPERHITS! (2001), touring as support to copyists Blink-182 and the subsequent abandonment of CIGARETTES AND VALENTINES in 2002 suggested that as a musical engine Green Day were running out of steam.

1998

JANUARY: 'GOOD RIDDANCE (TIME OF YOUR LIFE)'

Billie Joe had actually written the acoustic 'Good Riddance' back in 1993 after his relationship with his first serious girlfriend Amanda ended. This bittersweet song was released as a single and, as well as becoming a hit, crossed over into a wider cultural arena, where it was used to highlight clips on the last show of the highly successful SEINFELD series. Some hardcore punks saw this track as the ultimate Green Day sell-out whilst others saw this genre-breaking song as one of the greatest punk acts of all time. More importantly, it put Green Day back on the map (aided by some pyromania).

APRIL: CONTROVERSIAL TV APPEARANCE

During a five-date tour of Australia between 27 March and 4 April, Green Day had an interview-only appearance on Recovery TV, but when Billie Joe shouted, 'do you want to hear a song?' a hardcore group of Green Day fans screamed an affirmative answer. Taking instruments from the house band and ignoring the irate presenter, Billie Joe launched the band into a spirited version of 'The Grouch', the lyrics of which included several 'f***s'. When they had finished, Billie Joe strapped the guitar onto the back of the presenter, who was told to 'shut the f*** up' by Tre as he read out a list of their upcoming gigs. The band were then escorted out of the studio.

JUNE: KROQ WEENIE ROAST AND FIESTA

From Woodstock in 1994 (where he had a tooth knocked out) it seemed as if it were always Mike to draw the short straw. In 1997 he endured an elbow operation, the removal of wisdom teeth and separation from his wife. In June 1998 Green Day were playing at Los Angeles radio station KROQ's annual Weenie Roast Festival where they were second on the bill to The Prodigy. During Green Day's set, Third Eye Blind's bassist Arion Salazar ran onto the stage and bear-hugged Dirnt. Dirnt later confronted Salazar backstage and either Salazar or a Third Eye Blind fan threw a beer bottle, fracturing Dirnt's skull. Dirnt made a full recovery and no charges were pressed.

SEPTEMBER: MTV VIDEO MUSIC AWARDS

In September, Green Day's 'Good Riddance (Time Of Your Life)' won the MTV Video Music Award for Best Alternative Video. Also nominated were Radiohead's 'Karma Police', Ben Folds Five's 'Brick', The Verve's 'Bittersweet Symphony' and Garbage's 'Push It'. After it was announced that they had won, the band took to the stage to accept the award. Tre, dressed in tartan shorts and sporting green hair, breathed 'no way!' into the microphone, before Billie Joe stated, 'my wife's at home, she's having a baby next week so I want to say hi to her,' before thanking everyone from their managers to the director of the video, Mark Kohr.

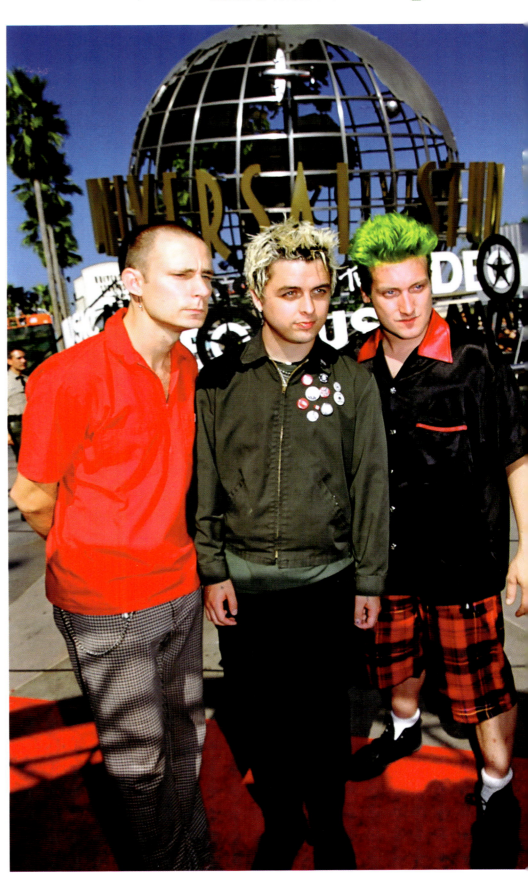

2000

WINTER: AT A CROSSROADS

Despite 'Good Riddance (Time Of Your Life)' making inroads to a new demographic, **INSOMNIAC** and **NIMROD** only sold around 3.5 million copies each worldwide. With Green Day copyists such as Blink-182 growing in popularity, the Bloodhound Gang finally gaining traction and Britpop and rap ever present on MTV, it was generally felt that Green Day were no longer musically relevant. Some reviews of **NIMROD** were caustic: **MELODY MAKER** was one example, stating 'With Green Day, there's a whole lot of nothing going on.'

FEBRUARY: PRODUCER UPHEAVAL

As producer and friend, Rob Cavallo had been pivotal in **DOOKIE**, **INSOMNIA** and **NIMROD** but the band thought change might stimulate their next album and turned to Scott Litt who had been crucial in delivering R.E.M's finest work. Litt saw the band perform their first acoustic-only set at Neil Young's Bridge Street fundraiser project and told **ROLLING STONE**, 'I'm excited about the album, some of the songs I've heard are really special.' Sadly, Litt was not special enough and failed to gel with the band, who elected to take full production duties themselves, with Cavallo acting in an executive role.

SPRING: MAKING A STATEMENT

Although Mike Dirnt was a massive collector of original punk seven-inch singles, what Billie Joe listened to filtered into his songwriting. His investigation of early Bob Dylan albums like BRINGING IT ALL BACK HOME (1965) certainly helped shape the long sessions for the new album. The track 'Hold On', dominated by acoustic guitar and harmonica, also had elements of Welsh band The Alarm blended into an energetic delivery. 'I don't want to become the type of band where people know what they're going to get from us before they hear it,' Billie Joe told KERRANG! magazine when discussing the sessions.

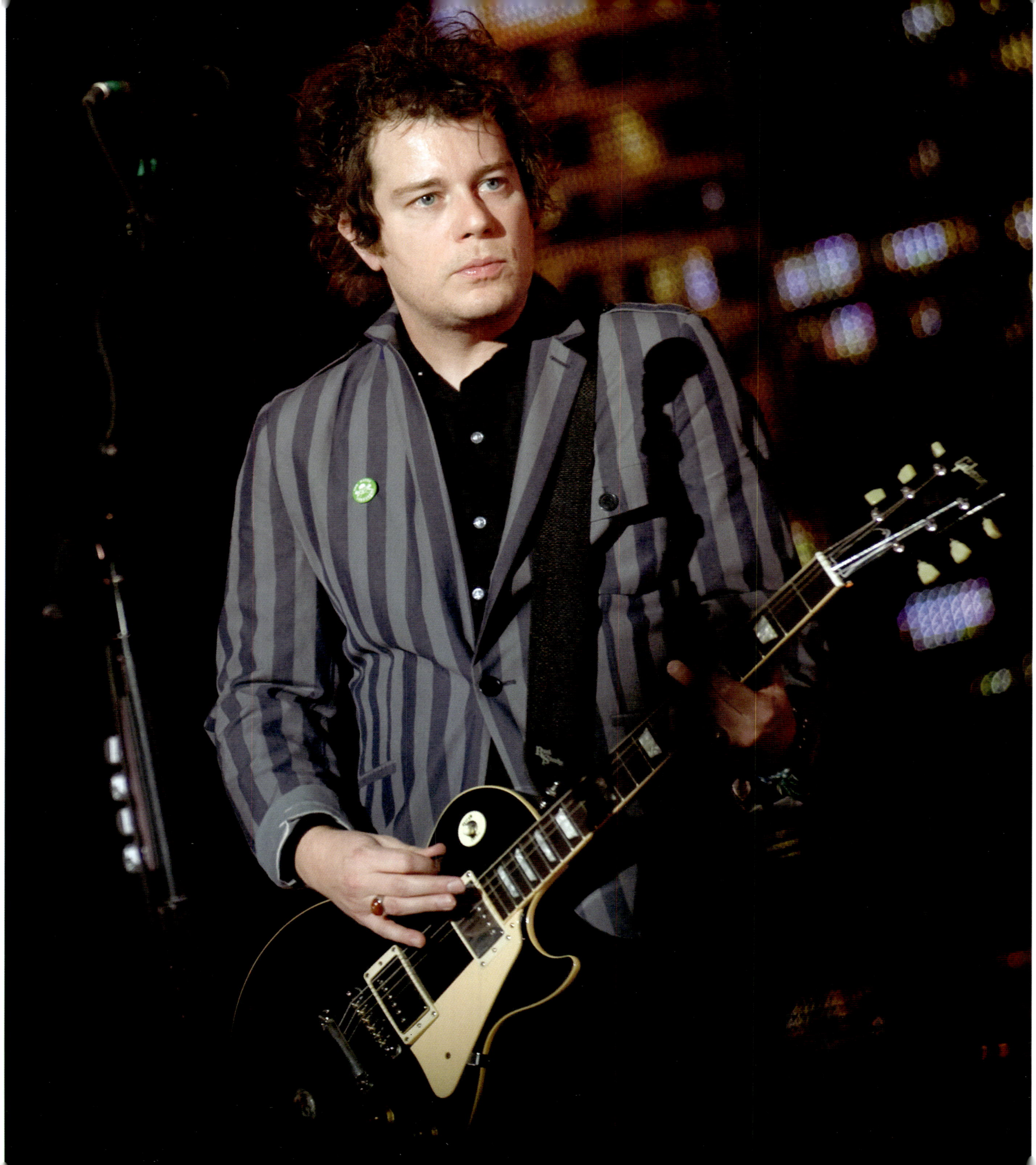

SUMMER: HEADLINE THE WARPED TOUR

With their sixth album in the can, Green Day went out on the road in the summer to headline the annual Warped Tour. Sponsored by the shoe manufacturer Vans, the first tour had taken place in 1994, and took a broad spectrum of punk and punk-skate bands around America; by 2000 it was an annual affair. Although eyebrows were raised about Green Day touring with a festival of – mostly – unknown bands, the 30 dates between 24 June and 6 August allowed them, augmented by second guitarist Jason White, to deliver a set of hard-hitting old favourites to outdoor audiences of between 5,000 and 10,000 people.

OCTOBER: 'MINORITY'

'I want to be the minority/I don't need your authority.' Billie Joe sings at the opening of this first Green Day protest song which was the lead single from new album **WARNING**. It was guided onto MTV by a promotional video that saw the band playing the song on a float as part of a Green Day parade through the streets of New York. Although the band sound more like The Alarm, the song showed Billie Joe looking outside of traditional Green Day lyrical concerns to areas like the 2000 American Presidential race between George W. Bush and Al Gore for immediate lyrical inspiration.

OCTOBER: WARNING

Although **WARNING** was in and out of the charts in pretty short order, in retrospect it was a pivotal album as it saw Green Day breaking away from perceived formulaic punk-rock templates. Although there was recognized Green Day fodder on tracks like 'Church On Sunday' and 'Misery', there was mature reflection from the acoustic strut of the title track – complete with air raid sirens – to the uplifting, wide-angled 'Macy's Day Parade', whilst 'Hold On' and 'Minority' gained traction amongst fans after repeat plays. 'We took a left turn,' a tight-lipped Billie Joe told **KERRANG!** in the wake of poor sales, but in time it proved to be the right one.

NOVEMBER: MILLION BAND MARCH

At the end of the Warped Tour, Green Day went back out on the road to promote **WARNING** around Europe, America and the Far East. They also played a free open-air concert on 5 November in San Francisco as part of a campaign against the gentrification of the Mission district of the city that was pricing artists and musicians out. Also on the bill was former Dead Kennedys' frontman Jello Biafra, singer-songwriter Victoria Williams and public speakers Metallica's Kirk Hammett and Democrat Tom Ammiano. There was a march prior to the show, although a million bands did not take part.

2001

APRIL: CALIFORNIA MUSIC AWARDS

Whilst their critical stock may have been low in other territories, it remained high in the Bay Area. This was confirmed when Green Day won eight statuettes at the annual California Music Awards (formerly the Bammies) held in Oakland on 24 April, hosted by Huey Lewis. **WARNING** won Outstanding Album, and Outstanding Punk Rock/Ska Album; Green Day won Outstanding Group and Outstanding Artist; Mike Dirnt won Outstanding Bassist; Tre Cool won Outstanding Drummer. Although Billie Joe won Outstanding Songwriter (beating Neil Young and Aimee Mann) and Outstanding Male Vocalist, the Outstanding Guitarist award went to Tom Morello from Rage Against The Machine!

JULY: CBGB

Green Day arrived at New York's CBGB club, made famous by punk rock, to watch a friend's band play. After a huge amount of drink, they rushed the stage at midnight and, deploying borrowed instruments, had the time of their lives playing the legendary venue. 'This is our first show ever here at the CBGB club,' Billie Joe announced, halfway through 'Scattered'; the set-list was a seat-of-the-pants affair but included 'Longview', 'Welcome To Paradise', 'She', 'Minority' and a number of covers, including a choice version of The Undertones' 'Teenage Kicks', punctuated by a fair amount of hardcore belching (from the band).

AUGUST: GIG ON THE GREEN FESTIVAL

The Gig On The Green Festival 2001 was held on 25 and 26 August in Glasgow, Scotland. The line-up included bands and artists that had supplanted Green Day in indie popularity, such as The Strokes, or in sales, such as The Queens Of the Stone Age, Marilyn Manson and new white rap sensation Eminem. Green Day rushed up to Scotland to perform after having appeared on Reading Festival's main stage the previous day. Their pert 13-song Reading set was flavoured strongly with old favourites like 'Longview', 'Welcome To Paradise' and 'Basket Case'.

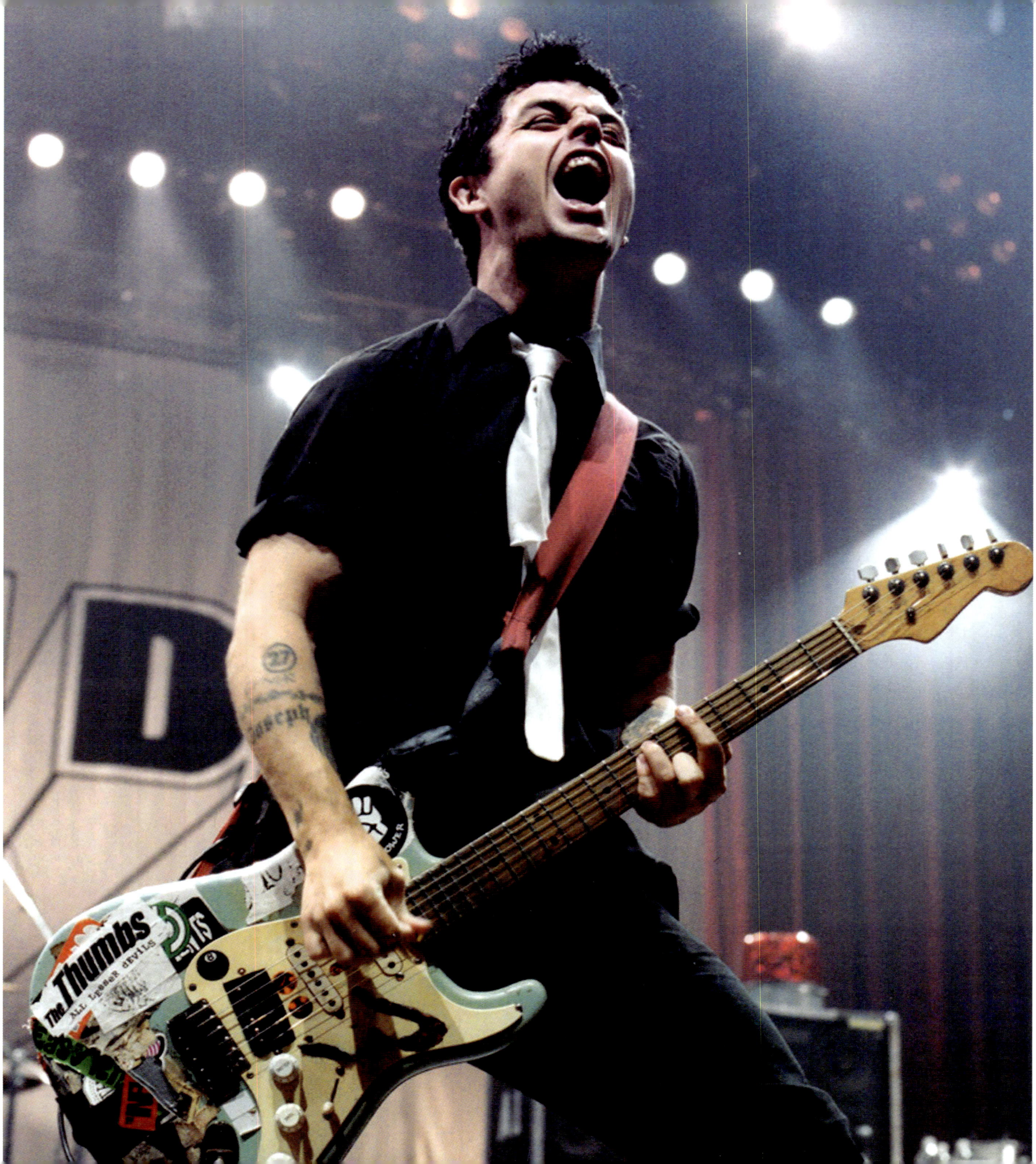
The Thumbs
ALL LESSER dEVILS

NOVEMBER: INTERNATIONAL SUPERHITS!

Released in November, **INTERNATIONAL SUPERHITS!** was a chirpy summation of Green Day's finest chart moments, showcasing hits ranging from 'Longview' to the less chart-adhesive 'Warning'. Two previously unreleased tracks, 'Maria' and 'Poprocks & Coke', opened the album; the track 'J.A.R. (Jason Andrew Relva)', which had appeared in the soundtrack to the film **ANGUS** (1995), also had its first outing. 'J.A.R.' was about Mike Dirnt's close friend who had died in a car crash; this event had prompted Dirnt to acquire a tattoo identical to one that Jason had: a snake wrapped around a dagger with the word 'brother'.

2002

SPRING: POP DISASTER TOUR

DOOKIE spawned a number of Green Day imitators such as Blink-182, who scored hit singles including 'What's My Age Again?'. Green Day shocked everyone by co-headlining with Blink-182 on the 42-date Pop Disaster Tour in America in April and May 2002. 'I think we've had a broader experience,' Billie Joe told **ALTERNATIVE PRESS**, 'we've played the biggest places in the world, and we've also played squats and the biggest toilets in the world. I think we kind of come from something a little more grassroots, DIY'. Green Day also got the last laugh as where they blew Blink-182 off the stage every night.

SPRING: GETTING AWAY FROM IT ALL

With no new Green Day album since **WARNING**, Billie Joe felt pressure to write new material. In order to get some head space he went alone to New York, renting an East Village apartment with the plan of writing new songs. He ended up spending quality time in bars and drinking or jamming with Ryan Adams who was also rediscovering his muse. 'I imagined that Ryan was your "perfect mess",' Billie Joe told **SPIN**,' but he was dropping names of Green Day songs I'd not heard since I was 16. We were f***ed up the entire time.'

JULY: SHENANIGANS

Whilst **INTERNATIONAL SUPERHITS!** collected Green Day's memorable and affirmative songs, this collection of B-sides, covers, soundtrack material and sundries showcased their diversity. Whilst there were great cover versions of The Ramones' 'Outsider' and 'I Want To Be On TV' by Fang, Green Day's take on The Kinks' 'Tired Of Waiting For You' indicated a shared melodic affinity which was affirmed on Billie Joe's 'Rotting'. 'Don't Want To Fall In Love' sounded like The Alarm jamming with The Clash with Duane Eddy taking a solo, whilst Mike Dirnt's 'Ha Ha You're Dead' was classic Green Day. 'On The Wagon' was surprisingly Bolan-esqe.

SEPTEMBER: MIKE UNDERGOES SURGERY

'I think he's gonna be fine. Everything was really smooth and he should be well pretty soon.' Billie Joe stated on 17 September in a press release. Mike Dirnt had undergone specialist surgery on his left wrist for carpal tunnel syndrome. This condition is caused by the compression of a nerve in the wrist which causes pain in the forearm and thumb and fingers, and is common to industrial workers on assembly lines, factory employees or men twanging bass guitars for Green Day. Mike made a full recovery in eight weeks.

NOVEMBER: CIGARETTES AND VALENTINES

'Expect straight-up rock'n'roll music.' Billie Joe told a journalist just before Green Day submerged to record the follow-up to **WARNING**. It was not until the 21st Century Breakdown Tour of 2009/10 that Green Day fans got to hear songs like 'Olivia' and the title track that were due to appear on their aborted seventh album **CIGARETTES AND VALENTINES**. After long and difficult recording sessions, the master tapes allegedly were stolen from the studio before they could be delivered to Reprise; although there were backups it was decided to abort the project and not re-record the songs.

RETURN TO FORM: 2003–05

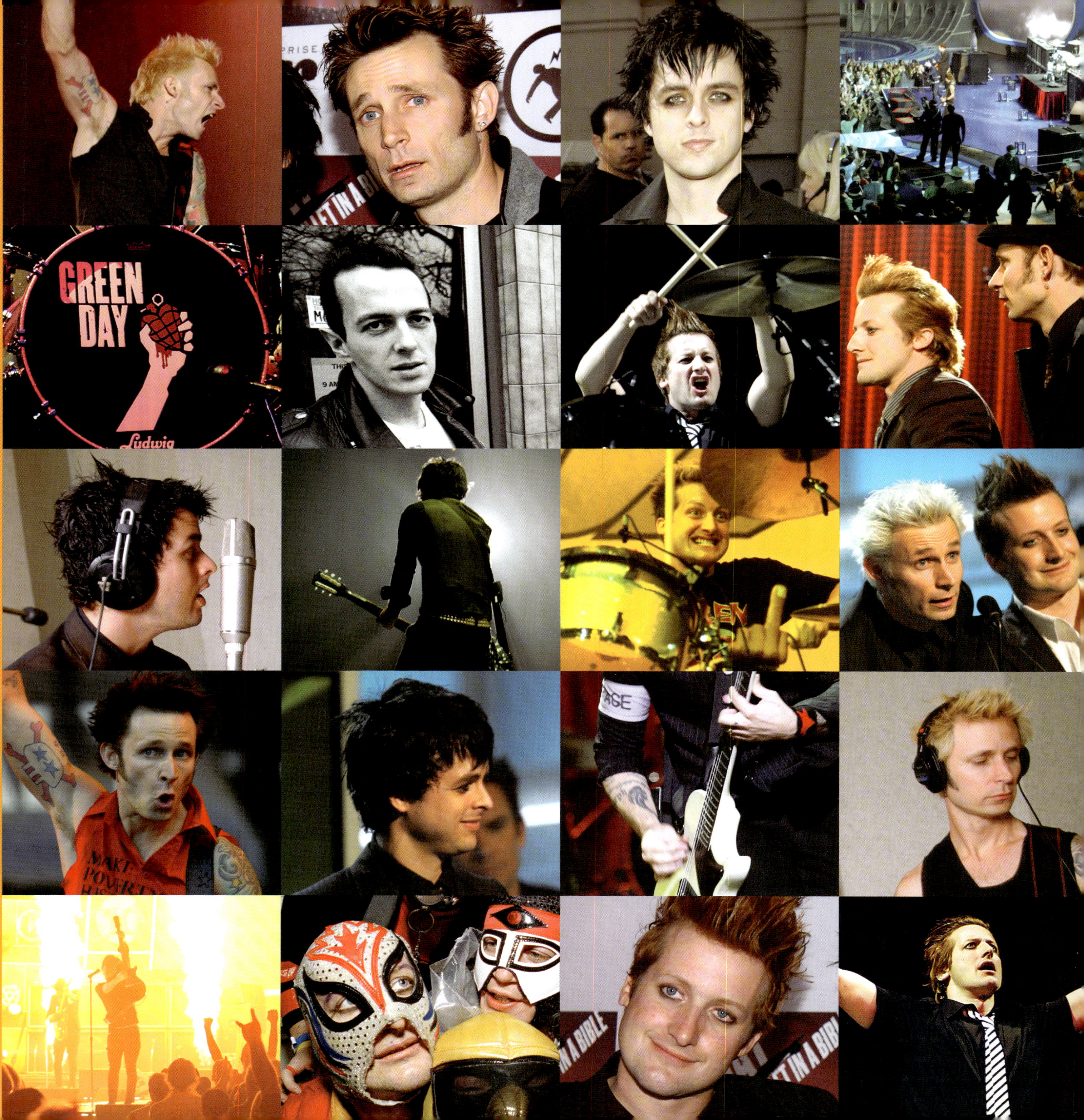

2003-05

The abandonment of CIGARETTES AND VALENTINES coupled with the arrant pleasure of recording as fictional band The Network restored Green Day's creative juices.

A subsequent studio experiment led the band on to craft their next album: a full-length, punk-rock opera, AMERICAN IDIOT (2004), which, armed with a political and sonic edge, catapulted them back into the big time. The album took a bold stance, questioning America's involvement in the Iraq war, the Republican agenda and Billie Joe's own feelings about his country; the songs were compelling: 'American Idiot', 'Holiday' and 'Wake Me Up When September Ends' all resonated not only in America but internationally. Supplemented with additional musicians, pyrotechnics and epic concert staging, Green Day returned to stadiums, delivering shows that were greeted with rapture by old and new fans alike. Like U2, Radiohead and Iron Maiden, Green Day were now international rock stars.

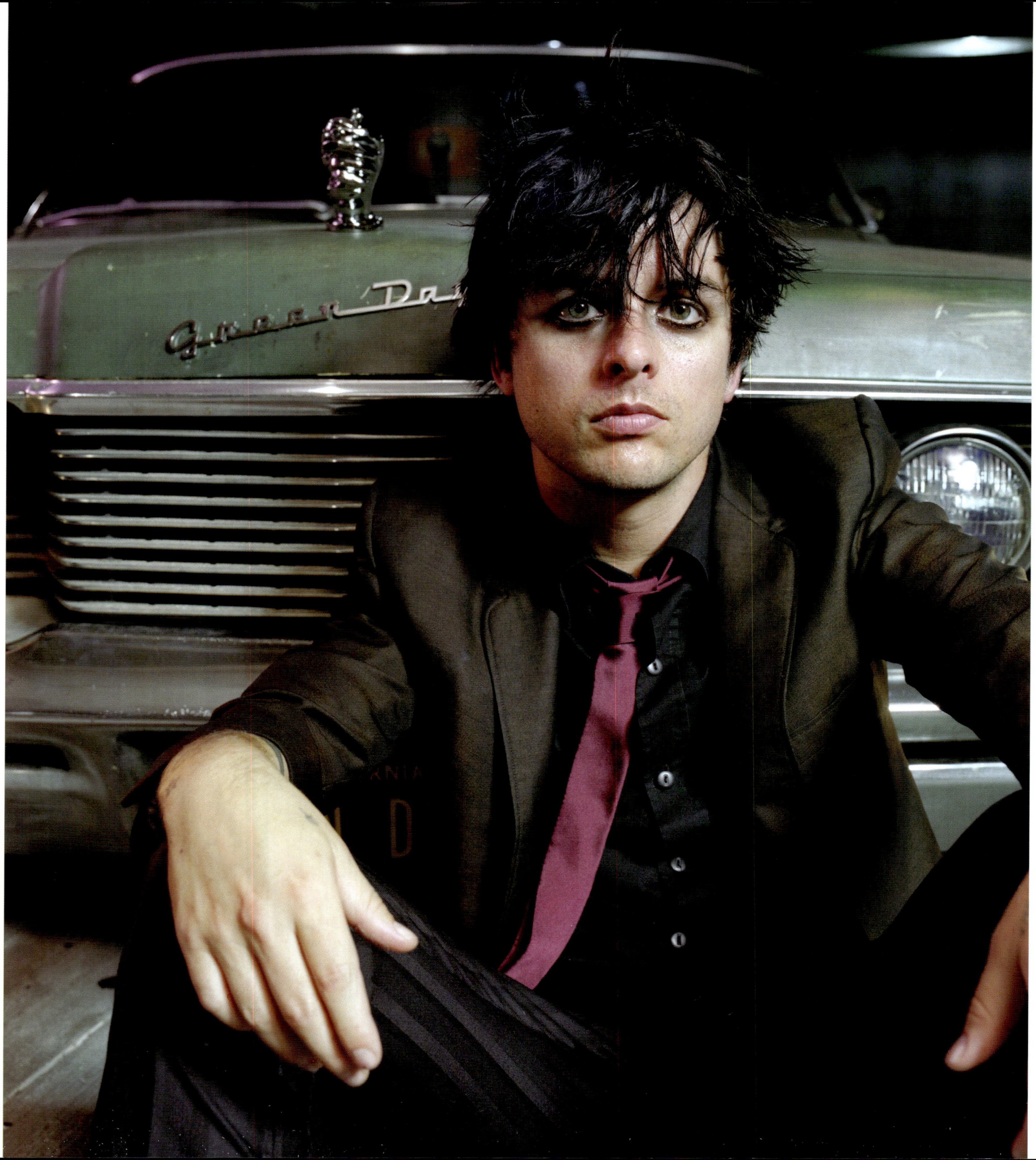

2003

JANUARY: BILLIE JOE'S DUI

'Let's get drunk and go out driving/Let's see how quickly we can go,' Tre Cool's track 'DUI' was supposed to be on SHENANIGANS but did not appear on the CD. Whether or not Billie Joe was listening to 'DUI' at 1am on 5 January when powering along in his BMW is unknown but he was stopped by police, breathalysed and booked for driving while twice over the California state legal limit. The story was quickly picked up by MTV news and even today the picture taken at the police station ranks amongst the Top 10 celebrity mug-shots.

SPRING: UNDER PRESSURE

The abandonment of CIGARETTES AND VALENTINES was, in retrospect, a watershed in the history of Green Day as it allowed the band to undertake a radical musical transition. At the time, however, it appeared to the press and public at large that the band had run out of creative steam and were coming to the end of the road. INTERNATIONAL SUPERHITS! and SHENANIGANS could have served as career-ending buffers with the band deciding to throw in the towel, step back from the limelight and live the good life of former rock-stars after over ten years in the field.

SPRING: THE CHALLENGE

'Everyone left the studio/Everyone left the studio/But m-e-e-e-e,' sang Mike Dirnt in a 30-second song fragment thrown together when his bandmates were absent. Tickled when he heard it, Billie Joe added his own section, Tre pitched in and over the following week an extended piece entitled 'Homecoming' developed. Initially they joked about the absurdity of a punk band moving into rock opera but when Rob Cavallo enthused about a rough mix, Green Day knew they were onto something. Significantly, they loved doing it and when Billie Joe – like Peter Townshend before him – thought of a story, they were off....

SUMMER: A EUROPEAN DIVERSION

Green Day cleared their musical block by throwing the rule book out of the window by going into Studio 880 in Oakland to record tracks as synth-rock outfit The Network. Signed to Billie Joe's Adeline Records, the five-man line up – Fink, Z, Captain Underpants, Van Gough and The Snoo – wore masks (like Slipknot, but less harrowing), suitably colourful clothing and concocted a band history that matched The Dukes Of Stratosphear and The Residents for invention. It involved stolen nuclear money, vegetarianism, alleged Olympic medals, a Mexican wrestler and, to confirm his Eurotrash synth-rock credentials, Z 'played keyboards with one finger'.

SUMMER: PIRATE BROADCASTERS

Along with musical Networking – 'we became so creative we could have knocked out a record every day,' Mike Dirnt told SPIN in 2004 – Green Day enjoyed rock-star partying and fun times that extended to doing something The Clash wanted to do but only sang about: setting up a pirate radio station. Ad hoc and erratic, it broadcast from Studio 880 to the Bay Area with the band playing favourite tracks and making crank calls: 'Tre called this animal crematorium in Hawaii,' Dirnt related, 'and told them he'd lost his monkey. And he kept asking, "Have you seen any monkeys?"'

SEPTEMBER: MONEY MONEY 2020

The Network's gloriously *loose* album **MONEY MONEY 2020** was released in September 2003 where Devo were thrown into a mixer with bubblegum rock, a dash of Kraftwerk and all manner of salty lyrical concerns from masturbation ('Right Hand-O-Rama') to 24-hour catwalk patrols ('Supermodel Robots'). Accusations that The Network were, in fact, Green Day were batted away by spokesman Fink, accusing Green Day of plagiarism; Billie Joe stepped into the ring with tongue firmly in cheek, 'The only thing I can say is f*** you Network, bring it on.' The Network played live at minor shows and a number of Green Day concerts.

DECEMBER: RIDING IN VANS WITH BOYS

RIDING IN VANS WITH BOYS was a low-budget documentary made on the Pop Disaster Tour following support band Kut U Up. Although Green Day were tangential they were also present in this wonderfully put together view of the highs, lows and high jinx of a two-month, small arena tour with endless van banter, gay jokes, pyro soundchecks, revolving drum kits, backstage golf, drinking and inter-band bonding as well as insight into hard touring. Billie Joe was even filmed urinating against a wall and then giving the cameraman the thumbs up before walking straight onto stage. Rock and roll!

2004

SEPTEMBER: 'AMERICAN IDIOT'

The song that was to revitalize the career of Green Day was a protest against the war in Iraq promulgated by American president George W. Bush. With lines like 'Don't want to be an American idiot,' 'I'm not part of a redneck agenda' and 'now everybody do the propaganda' was a powerful anti-Bush statement. Musically, 'American Idiot' was energetic and compulsive and, despite some American radio censorship when released in September 2004, put Green Day back in the charts – worldwide. Green Day launched an anti-war petition on their website and Billie Joe was photographed with a 'stop the war' placard.

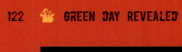

GREEN DAY.
PRESENTS
american
idiot

SEPTEMBER: AMERICAN IDIOT

'We've put everything on the line,' Billie Joe told the **NME**, 'we've put our career on the line for our point of view. By writing **AMERICAN IDIOT** we are putting our dookie on the line.' **AMERICAN IDIOT** was a concept album or 'punk opera' about a young boy, Jesus of Suburbia, leaving home on a journey of self-discovery in Bush's America and the people he meets: characters like the toxic St Jimmy and his nemesis Whatsername. Its musical cornerstones were the ambitious extended song cycles 'Jesus Of Suburbia' and 'Homecoming'. Reviews were gushing and sales monstrous, with the album topping the charts in America and the UK.

SEPTEMBER: RALLYING THE VOTERS

'I was actually a little disappointed about other people not stepping up,' Mike Dirnt told **NME** when discussing opposition to George W. Bush, Iraq and the 'redneck agenda' of the Republican party, 'Where's our Bonos or our Michael Stipes?' Actually Stipe, along with R.E.M., performed on the Pro-Senator Kerry Vote For Change Tour of October 2004, headlined by Bruce Springsteen, which targeted swing states and encouraged voter registration. Although not invited to perform (Billie Joe: 'they didn't go into our age group'), Green Day appeared and posed for photos with Kerry on David Letterman's **THE LATE SHOW** on 20 September.

NOVEMBER: 'BOULEVARD OF BROKEN DREAMS'

'Boulevard Of Broken Dreams' was the second single from AMERICAN IDIOT and the promotional video, directed by Samuel Bayer, intercut scenes of the band prowling desolate American countryside and a down-at-heel Los Angeles as Billie Joe sang with the band energetically performing the song in a warehouse. This powerful anthem gave Green Day their highest chart placing in America when it hit No. 2 in December; it reached No. 5 in the UK. In 2006 it won a Grammy Award for Record of the Year, beating competition from Mariah Carey, Gorillaz, Gwen Stefani and Kayne West.

DECEMBER: CHANGING THE LOOK

On the Pop Disaster Tour, it was Blink-182's rotating drum solo that had the theatrical edge but AMERICAN IDIOT saw Green Day brand everything. Taking his cue from a lyric in 'She's A Rebel' ('heart like a hand grenade'), artist Chris Bilheimer designed an arresting image of a white hand clutching a red, heart-shaped hand grenade which served as the cover for AMERICAN IDIOT and stage-branded the upcoming AMERICAN IDIOT tour. Although Billie Joe favoured black shirts and thin ties, the band gave themselves a rock star make-over ranging from industrial eye-liner to Hedi Slimane-designed Christian Dior suits.

DECEMBER: VH1 BIG IN 04

Music video channel VH1's third award show was held at the Shine Auditorium, Los Angeles, on 1 December, featuring awards from Biggest Catchphrase of 2004 ('That's Hot' Paris Hilton) to Biggest Musical Artist (Usher). Live music was provided by The Black Eyed Peas, Velvet Revolver and Green Day, who also performed at the Billboard Awards ceremony at the MGM Grand Garden Arena, Las Vegas, on 8 December, where Usher was voted the Best Artist – again!

2005

FEBRUARY: GRAMMY AWARD FOR BEST ROCK ALBUM

At the 47th Grammy Awards held on 13 February in Los Angeles, Green Day not only won Best Rock Album award for **AMERICAN IDIOT** but had their performance of the title track introduced by acclaimed film director Quentin Tarantino. Tarantino paid the band the ultimate compliment, stating that they had 'released a concept album with a very novel concept: all the songs are good.' The band lost out on Best Song for 'American Idiot' and Best Album to the late Ray Charles who had sadly passed away the previous year.

MARCH: 'HOLIDAY'

AMERICAN IDIOT catapulted Green Day to the top of the rock pecking order with mass coverage and interviews in publications from **NME, Q, ROLLING STONE** and **SPIN** to **TIME**. Every MTV operation in the world threw awards at them, including MTV Europe. At the awards ceremony in Lisbon they performed 'Holiday' and won Best Album and Best Rock Band, beating off stiff competition from U2, Foo Fighters, Franz Ferdinand and the not-so-stiff Coldplay. The band won around 41 awards in 2005, including **KERRANG!'S** Best Live Band and also their Best Band On The Planet award.

APRIL: VH1 STORYTELLERS

'It started with the basis of the story [of **AMERICAN IDIOT**] is three main characters. It takes place in this heightened political time and it's an emotional roller coaster,' Mike stated at the opening of Green Day's VH1 Storytellers' performance, broadcast in April. The band was interviewed prior to performing **AMERICAN IDIOT** live, giving insight into the genesis of their punk-rock opera. 'There is a conscious thing throughout the record,' Mike continued, 'and that it is speaking from an individual standpoint. It is not pointing fingers necessarily. It is direct though.'

SPRING: AMERICAN IDIOT WORLD TOUR

The American Idiot world tour kicked off with warm-up club dates like Bochum, Germany, on 1 October 2004. By the final gig on 17 December 2005 at the Telstra Dome in Melbourne, Australia, the band had performed around 154 shows to audiences of up to 65,000. With a massive lighting rig, video screens, additional musicians and pyrotechnics, the band paraded through **AMERICAN IDIOT** and past glories like 'Basket Case', 'Minority', 'Longview' and 'Brain Stew', as well as diverse cover versions including Queen's 'We Will Rock You', The Clash's 'I Fought The Law' and the Isley Brothers' 'Shout'.

JUNE: 'WAKE ME UP WHEN SEPTEMBER ENDS'

The ballad 'Wake Me Up When September Ends' was one of the most memorable songs on **AMERICAN IDIOT** and was released as the fourth single from the album in June 2005. The extended video, directed by Samuel Bayer, told the story of young American love. A couple's idyllic relationship is threatened when the boy joins the army to protect his girlfriend and his country. Scenes of Green Day performing the song are almost secondary to combat images in Iraq, interspersed with scenes of the girlfriend at home fearful for her lover's life which, when the song ends, is under direct threat.

JUNE: MILTON KEYNES BOWL

'Thank you,' Billie Joe screamed on 19 June at the end of a two-hour set, 'for being part of the biggest show that Green Day have ever played.' At that point the 65,000 people crammed into the Milton Keynes Bowl, England, roared their approval. That the band arrived by helicopter, laced two shows with pyrotechnics and ended their sets firing confetti onto the audience was only part of a spectacle where Billie Joe got a young boy on the stage to fire a water pistol and got a massive cheer when faking masturbation in the middle of 'Hitchin' A Ride'.

JUNE: ROSKILDE FESTIVAL

The **AMERICAN IDIOT** tour extended to a number of headlining European festival appearances in June and July that included Rock In The Park (Germany), Jammin Festival (Italy), Nova Rock (Austria), Interlaken (Switzerland), Nijmegen (Holland), Roskilde (Denmark), Oxygen Festival (Ireland) and T In The Park (Scotland). Musically, the band were on fire throughout, despite the fact that extended pieces like 'Homecoming' had required intense rehearsal to negotiate the various musical changes. Additional musicians like Jason White, Jason Freese, Mike Pelino and Rob Blake gave this new music dynamic punch and also allowed Billie Joe to play the front-man role to the hilt.

JULY: LIVE 8

Inspired by Live Aid, Live 8 was a direct response to the political G8 summit and an ambitious event that saw 10 concerts staged from London, England, to Johannesburg, South Africa, on 2 July to raise awareness about poverty and force politicians to act on pledges to cancel debts and assist the African continent. The event's slogan was 'make promises happen' and bands from a reconstituted Pink Floyd to the Pet Shop Boys performed. Green Day performed in Berlin, playing 'American Idiot', 'Holiday', 'Minority' and ending their short set with a cover version of Queen's 'We Are The Champions'.

AUGUST: MTV VIDEO MUSIC AWARDS

At the annual MTV video awards on 28 August, Green Day opened the show, performing 'Boulevard Of Broken Dreams', which won seven awards including Best Direction, Best Editing and Best Cinematography. When collecting the Rock Video Of The Year award, the band negotiated a water arch before Billie Joe stated, 'Thanks a lot, it's great to know that rock music still has a place at MTV,' a sly dig at its championing of hip hop and rap. When collecting Video Of The Year, Mike Dirnt remembered 'our soldiers, let's bring them home safe.' 'American Idiot' won Viewer's Choice award.

AUGUST: THE LOOKOUT! ALBUMS

When Green Day moved from Lookout! to Reprise they allowed the small independent label rights to their first two albums which, after **DOOKIE**, helped bankroll an expansion that led to the signing of a raft of new bands and funded the bottom line for the next ten years. By 2005, however, bands like Anvil, Screeching Weasels, Riverdales and Enemy You took control of their back-catalogues due to the non-payment of royalties; on 1 August Green Day, who were owed a large sum, did the same. Lookout! still operates today as a small independent label.

OCTOBER: PERFORM LIVE ON AOL MUSIC

By 2005, the internet was playing a vital role, allowing fans to read about and download music, stream videos and visit websites dedicated to their favourite bands. One of the key online players in America at this time was AOL which, on 11 October, broadcast Green Day's concert at the Wiltern Theatre in Los Angeles live. This allowed fans across America to join the concert virtually on AOL Music and watch the band perform a 15-song set. The success of this broadcast saw AOL roll out further performances by artists in a similar league to Green Day, including Madonna.

NOVEMBER: BULLET IN A BIBLE

Bullet In a Bible was an audio-visual documentary of Green Day's iconic two shows at the Milton Keynes Bowl in England on 18 and 19 June. The DVD, directed by Samuel Bayer, not only captured these energetic performances but took the viewer behind the scenes. 'I am Green Day. That is me. That is my life,' Billie Joe stated before the opening credits. The way he worked the crowd – from shouting 'England' halfway through 'American Idiot' to donning a fake crown and ermine cloak at one point – showed a master of the rock-and-roll art.

DECEMBER: TELSTRA DOME

The last stop on the **AMERICAN IDIOT** tour was Australia. Green Day played two big shows at the Sydney Cricket Ground on 14 December and the Telstra Dome in Melbourne on the 17 December. This was their second swing through the region as the band had visited Australia on an earlier, far-eastern leg of the tour in March. Despite this being the end of the road, the band performed with their customary energy, pulling out all the stops, and including the now obligatory on-stage pyrotechnics, audience participation and an Australian-themed singalong led by Billie Joe.

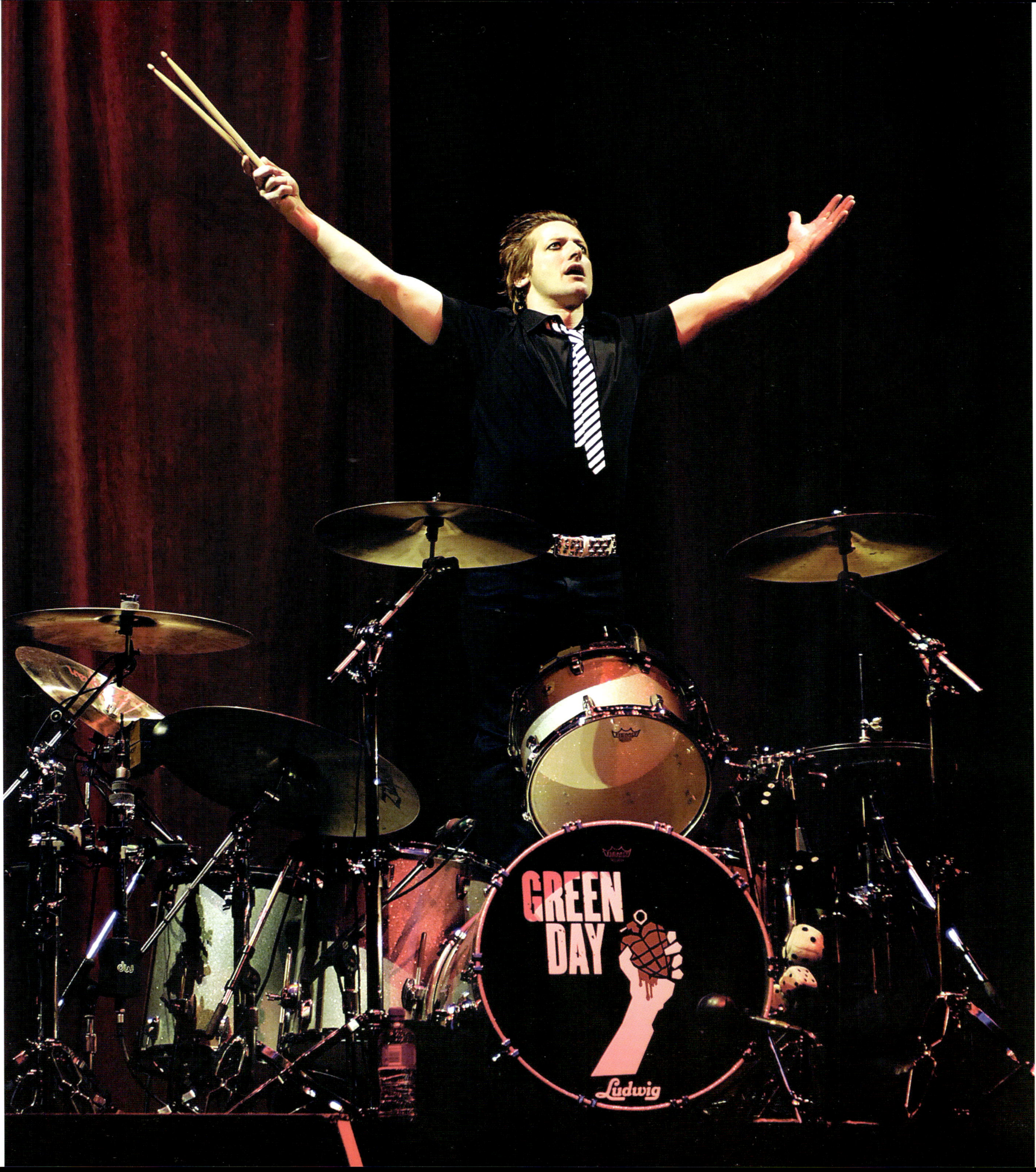
GREEN
DAY
Ludwig

DECEMBER: VH1 BIG IN 05

Green Day had appeared on the classic VH1 Storytellers format on 4 February in Los Angeles, playing the **AMERICAN IDIOT** LP before a small but delirious audience and also talking about the genesis of the concept, the meaning of the songs and what directly inspired them. They also attended VH1's Big in 05 show where they were even sent up – 'I walk a lonely street/probably because I wear eye liner' – but won the Big Music Artist award and, at the end of a short acceptance speech after receiving a very large trophy, Billie Joe stated, 'Holy pop culture, thank you.'

DECEMBER: IMPACT OF AMERICAN IDIOT

When examining the Green Day phenomenon, the media left no stone unturned, with features ranging from early Gilman Street days, punk specials and instrumental preferences to a four-page spread on the customized 1968 Mercury Monterey classic car that featured in the 'Boulevard Of Broken Dreams' and 'Holiday' promotional videos. 'It's been such a good year, it's weird,' Billie Joe understated to **ZERO** magazine in December 2005, 'We're in another place now,' chipped in Dirnt, 'and at this point Green Day is synonymous with good music and not just awards. **AMERICAN IDIOT** has started an entirely new chapter for this band.'

BROADENING HORIZONS: 2006–PRESENT

2006– PRESENT

AMERICAN IDIOT and 21st CENTURY BREAKDOWN (2009) cemented Green Day's position as one of the biggest, if not the biggest, rock band in the world. From their Hurricane Katrina collaboration with U2 to the honour of performing THE SIMPSONS MOVIE theme, Green Day were woven into the fabric of popular culture. Not only did more awards flow into their already large trophy cabinet but AMERICAN IDIOT translated into a Broadway musical, given additional traction by some appearances by Billie Joe in the production.

Green Day also enjoyed the thrill of their own computer game when they became only the second band – after The Beatles – to have a ROCK BAND release dedicated to their music. They also affirmed their reputation as one of the world's best live bands on stadium-sized concert tours which were captured in 2011 on the aptly entitled CD and DVD release AWESOME AS F**K.

2006

MAY: ASCAP POP MUSIC AWARDS

The American Society of Composers, Authors and Publishers (ASCAP) is vital in protecting the rights of artists such as Green Day by licensing public performances of their songs through mediums like radio and distributing royalties to songwriters. The ASCAP holds an annual awards ceremony to honour the most-performed songs in their repertory, and in 2006 Green Day'was also given the Creative Voice Award for their outstanding contribution to music. 'My best advice is to play music with your friends…' said Billie Joe when accepting the award, 'As,' Mike chipped in, 'you are guaranteed a good time.'

SEPTEMBER: HURRICANE KATRINA COLLABORATION

In 2005, Hurricane Katrina devastated the south-eastern seaboard of America and the historic city of New Orleans was flooded, leaving many residents homeless. When the football stadium, the Louisiana Superdome, reopened on 25 September for the New Orleans Saints' first home game, Green Day and U2 banded together as a seven-piece to deliver a four-song, half-time set to a crowd of 65,000. One of the songs was a cover version of Skids' 1978 apt song about storms and flooding, 'The Saints Are Coming', which was released as a collaborative single to raise money for the musical charity, Music Rising, in New Orleans.

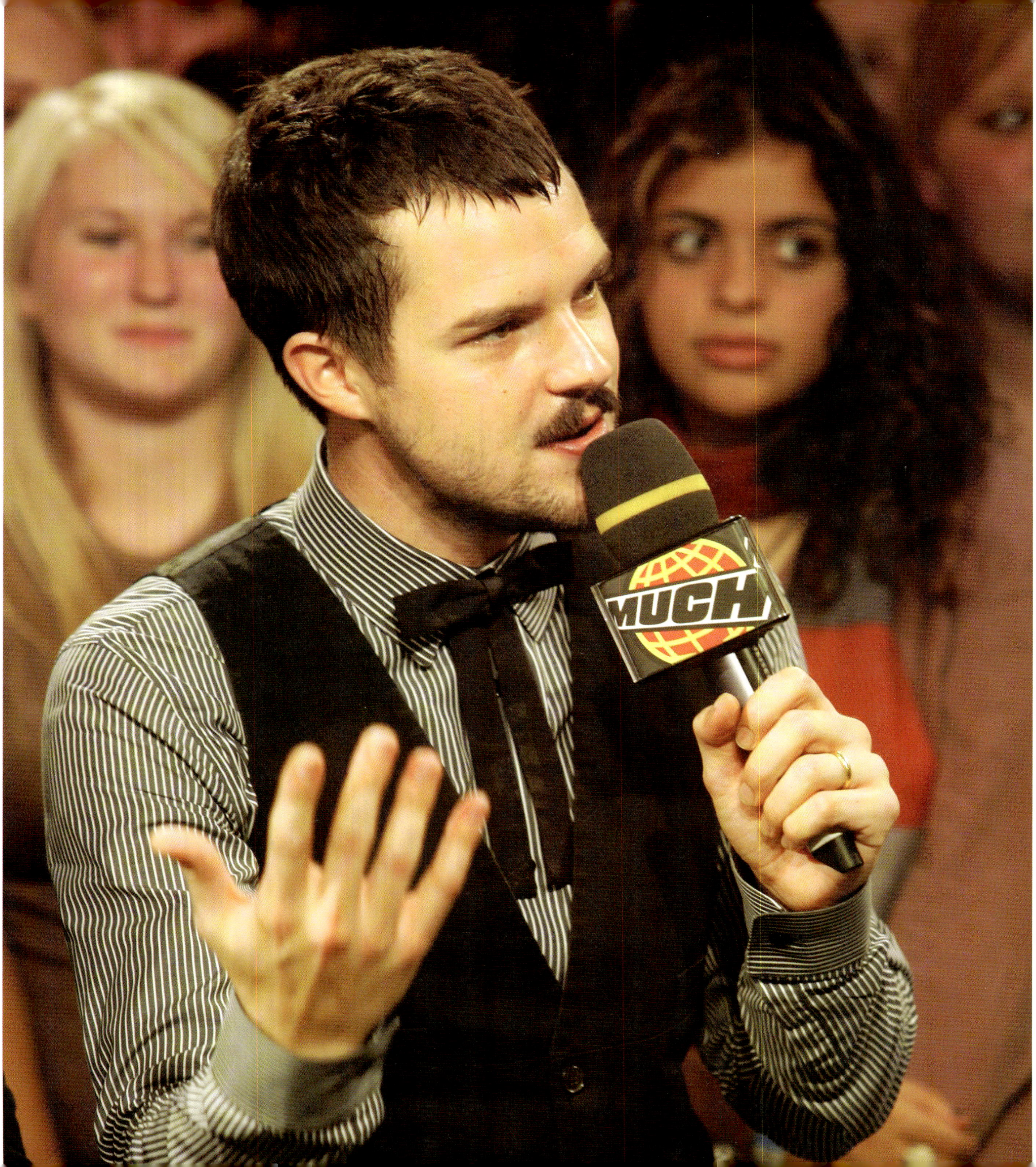
MUCH

OCTOBER: ANTI-AMERICAN ACTIVITY

The sentiments expressed on **AMERICAN IDIOT** pushed Green Day into the political arena, especially after stating their opposition to the American-led Iraq war. The band were always sure to stress in interviews that they were not anti-American (contrary to accusations made by The Killers' lead singer Brandon Flowers in October 2006) but more anti-Bush and the right-wing, fundamentalist views that he represented. 'Look, if Bush is morally and politically right, then I was screwed from the get-go,' Mike explained to **ROLLING STONE**. 'I come from a world he couldn't ever understand. Drugs and fighting and divorce.'

DECEMBER: REPRISE REISSUE

'There's moments in the show now when we go into 'Longview',' Mike Dirnt told a journalist in 2005, 'and while a lot of people still know it, there's a lot of people out there now that are like "What's this?" It was when that was happening that we knew we'd stepped out of the shadow of **DOOKIE** entirely.' Thus when Reprise reissued the first two Lookout! albums in December 2006, Green Day were more than happy to wax lyrical to journalists about the hard times of their spirited early years before **DOOKIE** turned their world upside down.

2007

JUNE: LENNON'S 'WORKING CLASS HERO'

In June 2007, the album **INSTANT KARMA** was released to raise money for the Amnesty International campaign to raise money to help those caught up in the conflict in Darfur, Sudan. The album featured covers of John Lennon songs performed by various artists, ranging from Aerosmith's take on 'Give Peace A Chance' to Green Day performing 'Working Class Hero'. 'Its themes of alienation, class and social status really resonated with us,' stated Billie Joe, 'It's such a raw, aggressive song ... we felt we could really sink our teeth into it.' The band had to pre-record the song for broadcast on the final of **AMERICAN IDOL** on 23 May, as producers were terrified that Billie Joe would swear on live TV.

DECEMBER: FOXBORO HOT TUBS

Before writing and recording a follow-up to **AMERICAN IDIOT**, Green Day created another side-project called the Foxboro Hot Tubs. This band, named after one of Green Day's youthful hangout spots in their native Bay Area, appeared on the radar after setting up a MySpace page in October 2007 and a free six-track EP was available for download in December 2007. 'The only similarity between Green Day and Foxboro Hot Tubs is that we are the same band,' Billie Joe told **NME** in 2008. This extended to touring band members Jason White, Jason Freese and Prima Donna frontman Kevin Preston.

2008

MAY: STOP, DROP AND ROLL!!!

The debut album by the Foxboro Hot Tubs entitled **STOP, DROP AND ROLL!!!** was released in May 2008 and was supported by a short tour of eight small clubs in the Bay Area with $20 tickets only available on the night. Musically, the album dropped anchor in various ports of the 1960s with guitars, drums and bass supplemented by gloriously cheesy organ. 'Red Tide' sounded very much like The Kinks' 'So Tired' whilst 'Mother Mary' had the modern friction and panache of The Strokes. Like The Network, the Tubs had a fictional history supplementing club dates, on occasion, by supporting Green Day.

OCTOBER: BUTCH VIG SIGNS UP

'Right now, it's that no pressure/fun stage of just getting on a four-track and coming up with some goofy stuff,' Billie Joe told **BILLBOARD** magazine about writing songs for the new album, 'Eventually, something sort of unfolds.' What unfolded first was Green Day deciding to deploy former Garbage drummer Butch Vig as producer. Vig was best known for producing Nirvana's colossus **NEVERMIND** as well as The Smashing Pumpkins' **SIAMESE DREAM** (1998). Green Day confirmed the rumours by posting a 45-second video clip on the internet filmed by Vig who, after filming Billie Joe playing guitar, gave the viewers 'the finger'.

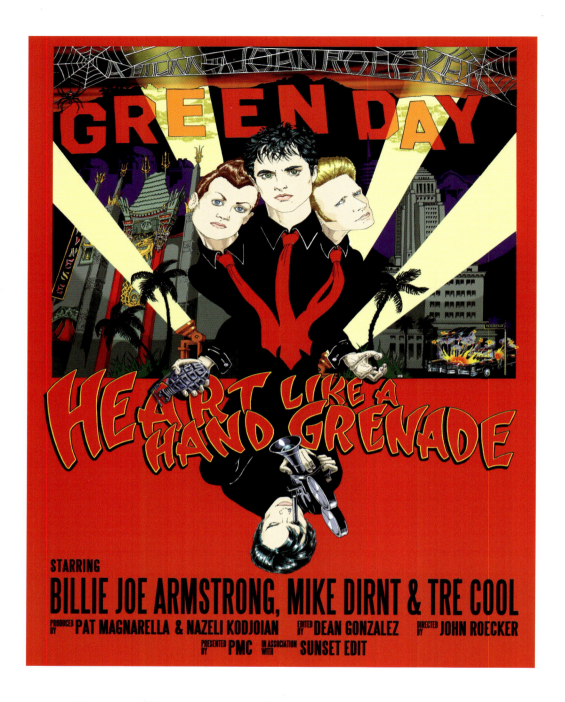

2009

MARCH: HEART LIKE A HAND GRENADE

Filmmaker and punk-rock fan John Roecker was given access at various stages of the recording of **AMERICAN IDIOT** and 300 hours of footage was eventually boiled down to a two-hour film entitled **HEART LIKE A HAND GRENADE**. Although completed, apart from some limited showings the film has yet to be officially released. Tantalizing clips on the internet range from a Tre Cool studio drum solo watched by Billie Joe who then deadpans, 'let's go shopping', via the serious business of laying down tracks, to Tre Cool giving expert advice on how not to get drunk (drink water between beers).

MAY: 21ST CENTURY BREAKDOWN

The eagerly awaited follow-up to **AMERICAN IDIOT** entitled **21ST CENTURY BREAKDOWN** was another Green Day rock-opera. Divided into three suites, the plot revolves around the relationship between a punk-rock couple, Gloria and Christian, against a backdrop of a modern America, 'in a transition from one destructive era to something new.' The album ranges from spite against fundamentalist religion in the track 'East Jesus Nowhere', to the wonderfully Lennon-esque love song 'Last Night On Earth'.

MAY: PARENTAL ADVISORY

21st CENTURY BREAKDOWN received positive reviews, topping album charts worldwide and generally banishing any worry that there might be another post-DOOKIE comedown. In America, however, the largest retail outlet Wal Mart refused to stock the album due to their policy of not selling any CDs that carry 'parental advisory' stickers. The band were asked to provide the retailer with a version without offending language. 'There's nothing dirty about our record,' Billie Joe stated, 'They want artists to censor their records in order to be carried in there. We just said no. We've never done it before. You feel like you're in 1953 or something.'

MAY: GOOD MORNING, AMERICA

Green Day made a number of TV appearances to promote the release of 21ST CENTURY BREAKDOWN, although their reputation as America's No. 1 band commanded a live, four-song set at Rumsey Playfield, Central Park, New York, on the morning of 22 May that was broadcast live on ABC's GOOD MORNING AMERICA show. The band performed '21st Century Breakdown', 'Know Your Enemy', 'American Idiot' and 'Longview'; Billie Joe was interviewed live on stage and halfway through explaining the concept behind the album was asked a more important question by one of the presenters: 'How do you contain Tre?'

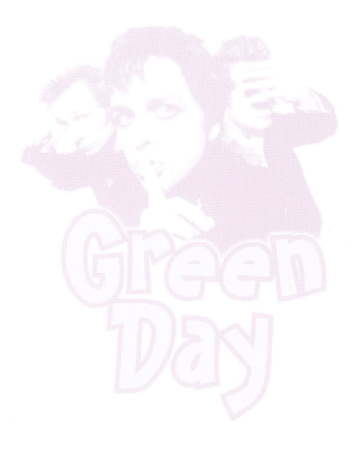

JUNE: HENRY FONDA THEATRE

After intense rehearsals, Green Day played a number of small warm-up dates in June 2009 for the 21st CENTURY BREAKDOWN tour. Their performance at the Henry Fonda Theatre in Los Angeles served up 12 songs from the new album, including a piece of theatre from Billie Joe on 'East Jesus Nowhere' where a young boy sang along with him which, for the world tour, translated into 'saving a child' from the audience on stage like a fundamentalist preacher. The second part of the performance saw the band play loudly old favourites suggested by the crowd, ranging from 'Longview' to the now obligatory 'American Idiot'.

JULY: WORLD TOUR BEGINS

The 21ST CENTURY BREAKDOWN tour officially kicked off in Seattle on 3 July 2009. After playing 37 stadiums in America and Canada, it moved to Europe and the Far East before ending at the Parc des Princes in Paris on 26 June 2010. The first part of the set was dedicated to BREAKDOWN before old favourites were unfurled. For pure theatre, the image of Billie Joe shining a torch into the audience during 'Holiday' before pronouncing, 'the representative of [insert name of city here] is in the building/Sieg Heil to the President Gasman' is one of the most iconic in modern music.

AUGUST: THE FORUM

Although they were now used to playing large arenas like The Forum, Los Angeles, on 25 August 2009 Green Day still worked hard to put on a good show. To keep things fresh they would sometimes dredge up gems from their past like 'Tight Wad Hill' or roll out a mind-boggling number of cover versions in their extended sets that ranged from the Buzzcocks' 'Ever Fallen In Love' via Billie Idol's 'Dancing With Myself' to Survivor's 'Eye Of The Tiger' which was played once with Billie Joe struggling to remember the lyrics: 'rising up – dah dah dah dah!'

SEPTEMBER: '21 GUNS'

The first single from 21st CENTURY BREAKDOWN was 'Know Your Enemy', released in May 2009 prior to the album launch; this was followed up by the power-rock ballad '21 Guns'. The video was directed by Marc Webb and scenes of the band performing the song (with Jason White as a fourth member) were intercut with scenes of the two characters from the album in a room being blasted by bullets; the video ends with the pair embracing, unharmed by the bullets, echoing the album's cover art. It won Best Rock Video at the 2009 MTV Video Music Awards, as well as Best Direction in a Video and Best Cinematography in a Video. Green Day performed 'East Jesus Nowhere' at the ceremony.

SEPTEMBER: AMERICAN IDIOT WORLD PREMIERE

When director Michael Mayer approached Green Day about the possibility of transferring **AMERICAN IDIOT** onto the stage, the band were shocked, but after seeing his award-winning play **SPRING AWAKENING** agreed. 'It's going to be my wildest dream,' Billie Joe told the **NEW YORK TIMES** in March 2009. **AMERICAN IDIOT** made its debut at the Berkeley Roda Theatre on 4 September 2009 and was a cogent, powerful rock-opera that brought the story of Johnny loudly to life, receiving excellent reviews. As well as using songs from **AMERICAN IDIOT**, Billie Joe helped Mayer work four songs from **21ST CENTURY BREAKDOWN** into the production.

OCTOBER: THE ART OF ROCK

To coincide with the UK leg of Green Day's **21ST CENTURY BREAKDOWN** tour, 21 artists were invited to produce work inspired by lyrics from the album. This was exhibited at the StolenSpace Gallery, Brick Lane, in London's East End between 23 October and 1 November 2009. Curator Logan Hicks served up striking portraits of the band set against red backgrounds; Sixten depicted a dove trying to pull the pin from a hand grenade and The London Police drew what looked like a tour-bus robot, controlled by Green Day, attempting to grab three Lego-like replicas of the band.

JUNE: WEMBLEY STADIUM

'Playing Wembley stadium is like one of those moments in your career when you just go "holy shit!"' Billie Joe stated when the band held a press conference at the London venue to announce their concert. Although the stadium capacity was 90,000, to accommodate the stage some seating was not used. On the day, Green Day played 39 songs to a wildly enthusiastic audience who also witnessed Tre on guitar and Billie Joe on drums for 'Dominated Love Slave', two encores and Billie Joe firing toilet rolls into the audience using a special hand-held machine.

NOVEMBER: MTV EUROPE MUSIC AWARDS

When arriving in Berlin for the 2009 MTV Europe Music Awards, Billie Joe told a news reporter that the European leg of the 21ST CENTURY BREAKDOWN tour had been their best ever, 'they're like the toughest crowds in the world but after a song and a half they are like butter in our hands.' The band was nominated in three categories but only won the award for Best Rock Album. Before playing 'Know Your Enemy' and 'Minority' Billie Joe got the audience going by screaming, 'everybody stand the f*** up, let's go!' U2 won the award for Best Live Act – just.

NOVEMBER: AMERICAN MUSIC AWARDS

Green Day were first nominated for Favourite Artist in the Alternative Rock Music category of the American Music Awards back in 1995 and, despite further nominations in 1996, 1998 and 1999, did not win until 2005 in the wake of **AMERICAN IDIOT**; they won for a second time on 22 November 2009. Billie Joe spoke about the importance of alternative and punk music when accepting the award, but at the press conference prior to the ceremony he had been thrown a strange question: 'why is music so important during the holidays?' 'Because it makes you forget that you have to shop,' was his quick-witted reply.

2010

JANUARY: GRAMMY FOR BEST ROCK ALBUM

'Is this old hat now?' an interviewer from **TV GUIDE** asked the band after **21ST CENTURY BREAKDOWN** won a Grammy for Best Rock Album, 'No, no, this is never old hat,' replied Billie Joe, 'when you put that much effort into a record nothing is old hat.' At this point a member of Kings Of Leon handed Billie Joe a hip flask from which he took an epic pull. 'Whisky?' quizzed Tre before taking a pull, 'Tequila!' he said post swig. Billie Joe suggested that Green Day and Kings Of Leon might trade shots a little later on.

MARCH: THE STOOGES' HALL OF FAME INDUCTION

The Stooges had been voted down a record six times for induction into the American Rock'n'Roll Hall Of Fame but were finally admitted in March 2010, along with Genesis and The Hollies. Billie Joe gave a five-minute speech: 'they symbolized the destruction of flower power and gave us raw power', before handing Iggy the award. When The Stooges cranked up 'I Wanna Be Your Dog', Billie Joe started on guitar but ended up with his arms wrapped around Iggy belting out the chorus as Tre, Mike and other members of the audience cavorted on stage.

APRIL: AMERICAN IDIOT HITS BROADWAY

After success in Berkeley, **AMERICAN IDIOT** transferred to Broadway, New York, where it opened at the St James Theatre on 20 April 2010. This 'story of American youth looking to improve their lives,' as director Michael Mayer aptly put it, received positive reviews, although it struggled to sell out every night. When Billie Joe stepped in to play the role of St Jimmy for one week between 28 October and 3 November, sales went through the roof. Billie Joe was to make many more appearances including a final three-week run before the show closed at the end of April 2011.

JUNE: GREEN DAY: ROCK BAND

The first **ROCK BAND** game dedicated to one artist featured The Beatles and on 8 June 2010 the second featured Green Day. 'They're a really good fit with **ROCK BAND** fans,' stated game producer Alan Moore, '**ROCK BAND** fans grew up with the band.' There was enormous attention to detail, with venues like the famed Milton Keynes Bowl being accurately rendered; individual band members were precisely depicted, right down to 'the collection of all the tattoos down the years,' stated Billie Joe. Fans could play 47 Green Day songs including the complete **AMERICAN IDIOT** album, **DOOKIE** and beyond.

JUNE: PARC DES PRINCES

One of Billie Joe's greatest achievements is the ability to turn the Roman/Nazi salute into a piece of rock theatre. At the sell-out concert at Paris's Parc Des Princes Stadium on 26 June when the band approached the famous breakdown segment in 'Holiday', the audience already had their arms up in anticipation; at this point Billie Joe took a musical sidestep into an *ad hoc* rendition of 'The Saints Are Coming' before returning to the 'Sieg Heil to the President Gasman,' in front of the outstretched arms of a *French* audience.

JUNE: TONY AWARDS FOR AMERICAN IDIOT

Although nominated for the Best Musical award at the annual Tony Awards held at Radio City Music Hall in June 2010, AMERICAN IDIOT lost out to the production of MEMPHIS although it did win two awards for Best Scenic Design and Best Lighting Design. At the awards ceremony, John Gallagher Jr and the cast performed the show's rendition of 'Boulevard Of Broken Dreams'; he then announced, 'from Oakland, California, my heroes: Green Day,' and the band appeared, delivering 'Holiday' and 'Know Your Enemy' with great panache and pyrotechnics for the somewhat bemused audience.

AUGUST: LOLLAPALOOZA FESTIVAL

The last time Green Day had performed on the Lollapalooza Festival was in 1994 when it had been a touring festival; they had travelled in their famed Bookmobile for one leg of the tour. From 2005 the festival had become a three-day event held in Chicago. Green Day headlined on the main stage at the 2010 festival on 7 August. They fired on all cylinders although, as always, songs like 'Wake Me Up When September Ends' were singalongs. The Strokes, Soundgarden, Arcade Fire, Lady Gaga and The National were also on a diverse stellar bill.

SEPTEMBER: SHORELINE AMPHITHEATRE

With this venue situated in the outskirts of their native Bay Area, Green Day's show at the Shoreline Amphitheatre on 4 September was a spectacular homecoming for the band. Billie Joe took delight in screaming to the crowd that he was 'Home! Home! I'm fucking home!' in a three-hour performance during which Green Day mined their archive to enthuse an audience of 22,000. Alongside the well-known, the band paraded a montage of cover versions that included AC/DC's 'Highway To Hell' and The Beatles' 'Hey Jude'; although it was summer, members of the support band AFI came on stage dressed as Santa and threw hotdogs out into the crowd. What a homecoming.

2011

JANUARY: AMERICAN IDIOT CELEBRATES 300TH SHOW

Billie Joe joined the cast of AMERICAN IDIOT on New Year's Day 2011 for 50 performances spread between January and February and so was on hand to celebrate its 300th performance on 8 January. He appeared with the cast in a photo call with a cake to mark the event. Plans were being hatched and auditions held for a touring version of the play and rumours that AMERICAN IDIOT would translate soon onto the big screen were confirmed in April 2011, with Tom Hanks signing on as producer of the project.

FEBRUARY: AMERICAN IDIOT GRAMMY WIN

Although **AMERICAN IDIOT** was to close on Broadway after some 421 performances on 24 April 2011, it spawned an original Broadway cast soundtrack album that was nominated for a Grammy in the Best Musical Show Album category. When the awards took place at the Staples Centre, Los Angeles, on 13 February, the soundtrack won the award. Although Green Day fans may have found it strange listening to other artists performing the band's songs, many bought the album that featured great performances from John Gallagher Jr, Rebecca Naomi Jones, Tony Vincent and Michael Esper.

MARCH: AWESOME AS F**K

On 21 March the live album and DVD AWESOME AS F**K was released internationally. It documented 17 songs performed on the 21ST CENTURY BREAKDOWN world tour of 2009/10 selected by the band at shows ranging from London ('21st Century Breakdown') via Berlin ('When I Come Around') to Australia ('She'). The accompanying DVD captured a show performed by the band in Saitama, Japan; in the wake of the terrible devastation wrought in Japan by the tsunami in March 2011, one Green Day website was quick to auction a signed Green Day ROCK BAND promotional photo to raise money for victims.

INDEX